HELL BENT

Mandy Lee

For all the spicy, snarky romantics out there.

xoxo

CHAPTER ONE

Devlin Laflamme sighed and pulled off her glasses, rubbing at her tired eyes. This contract was going to be the death of her. She set her glasses down beside her laptop and gave the offending document a withering glare. She was *not* going to be defeated by the mountain of amendments opposing counsel had red-lined. She flipped her laptop closed and spun in her chair to look out her office window.

You didn't get to be lead corporate counsel by giving up!

She had earned her corner office through years of late nights poring over deals to find the hidden potholes and tripwires laid by her counterparts. Devlin was a master at the art of contract writing – the devil was always in the details! Obsidian Enterprises was a family business, but her dad wasn't in the habit of doing anyone favors, his daughter included. She'd had to work like a dog every step of the way and was damned proud of her reputation as a legal shark.

She stood and leaned her forehead against the cool glass as she gazed out at the twinkling lights of the city. There was nothing quite like the sight of Toronto after dark. High-rises that seemed stark and forbidding during the day became magical towers of fairy lights stretching up into the clouds. Devlin loved driving home along the Gardiner Expressway after dark. For several kilometers the highway became an overpass that floated above the city roads, making her feel like she was flying in the dark among the lights of the buildings that sandwiched the road. Not to mention, at night she could really hit the gas and let her Audi tear along the open road, no rush-hour gridlock to be seen. There were some perks to being a workaholic, and she'd take that one for a win!

Devlin reluctantly turned away from her beloved city view. She reached down and grabbed her laptop case off the floor beside her desk. It was getting late, and she had a solid thirty-minute drive ahead of her. Wednesday night was her standing 8 pm. dinner date with dear old dad...not that many people thought of her dad as dear... or old for that matter. Damien Laflamme was the ultimate silver fox, tough-as-nails CEO. He prowled the office in his designer pinstripe suits looking like a billionaire gangster who'd slay you in the boardroom rather than gifting you cement shoes. He ripped competitors apart one business deal at a time and had fun doing it. He was protective, but tough on her, and Devlin loved him for it. She'd grown up with a strong sense of who she was and what she could accomplish if she put her mind to it. Her dad had raised her to be a strong and independent woman, but he'd made sure she always knew she was his princess.

She finished dumping her laptop, notebooks, mobile phone, and wallet back into her bag. By the time she was done loading her stuff up at the end of each day, she felt like she was lugging around an anchor. It was a wonder she wasn't a regular visitor at the local chiropractor. Devlin did a half-turn to give herself a once-over in the mirror on the opposite wall. She ran her fingers quickly through her wavy blonde hair. It wouldn't do to show up at dinner with a bird's nest on her head. She quickly ran her hands down her dress, tugging it gently to smooth out the creases. Red was her signature color, and it just made her life so much easier to have a closet full of it – every morning she could just reach in and grab whatever she touched first!

Satisfied that she didn't look like a total hot mess, Devlin shrugged on her coat and tossed her "everything but the kitchen sink" bag over her shoulder. She winced as she glanced down at her watch. *Shit, running late again.* One of dad's pet peeves was lateness. Well, they'd have plenty to discuss to distract him from that when he saw the mess opposing counsel had made of this contract.

There were so many red-lines on the document it looked like it was bleeding! Devlin thought she would literally go blind just trying to make sense of the damn thing. It looked like the owners of the company Obsidian Enterprises was trying to acquire had suddenly decided to start negotiating like the fate of the world depended on it. Weird, since they'd seemed *very* motivated to sell just a few short weeks ago. *Oh well,* she thought. She had plenty of notes to discuss with her dad over dinner. It really was time to get moving though... *Nobody* kept the Devil waiting, not even his daughter!

CHAPTER TWO

"What on earth does this prick think he's playing at?" Damien Laflamme growled as he pored over the contract they'd printed out from Devlin's laptop. She felt the temperature in the room rise a degree or two as her dad's frustration mounted. "The owners of Harvest Time Garden Market already agreed to the terms of sale at your last meeting, didn't they?"

Devlin sighed and nodded. "Yeah, we basically shook on a done deal. I went back to the office, put together a finalized copy of the sale agreement, and had it back to them within twenty-four hours."

Damien shook his head in disgust. "I remember the day when a verbal contract was binding. Sometimes I really miss the old ways."

"Dad, we can't exactly start torturing executives in the boardroom when they renege on a deal...well, not literally at least," Devlin said, rolling her eyes.

"Remind me why not," he muttered, angrily flipping the pages of the contract.

Devlin chuckled to herself. Her dad was a real

enigma. Evil...yes...a master manipulator...yes...putty in the hands of his only daughter...absolutely! She was the reason he'd left Hell in the hands of his right-hand demon and come to the human realm to found Obsidian Enterprises. Damien had met her mother on one of his bi-millennial vacations to the mortal realm. He'd been immediately smitten. He always told her that it was her mother that had shown him the true value of a soul...for when it found its mate, it made life worth living. When Devlin was born, their little family was complete and life was perfect...until her mother's illness. Devlin had only been five years old, but she remembered her dad's grief as though it was yesterday. Since his wife's death, he'd thrown himself into being a single dad and slaying in the boardroom.

"Oh, Dad, I know how hard it must be for you to stick to litigation instead of the rack." Devlin leaned in to give him a kiss on the cheek before turning and plopping down onto the plush couch. Her dad's study was "their" place. They'd each sit with a snifter of brandy from Damien's bar, Devlin on the leather couch, Damien in his throne-like wingback chair. They'd pore over business deals and discuss which company they should target for acquisition next. Lately, Damien had been cornering the organic grocery market, building up his empire, getting as close to a monopoly as he could get without running afoul of the competition bureau. The

Devil never did anything by half-measure; he was an all-or-nothing type of guy.

Harvest Time Garden Market was Damien's current prey. The family-owned, farm-to-table grocery chain had seen a drop in revenue since the death of president and family patriarch, George Webster. Infighting and squabbling among his children over who should take over had led to confusion, unpaid vendors, dwindling customer satisfaction, and plummeting revenues, making it ripe for someone like Damien to come along with a purchase offer. Two weeks ago, when Devlin had negotiated the final sale conditions, she thought this would be all wrapped up in a nice little bow, but suddenly an estranged family member had cropped up out of nowhere to throw a wrench into the deal. Daniel Webster was an heir to the business...but annoyingly, he was also proving to be a damned fine lawyer. He had somehow managed to find fault with every clause she'd written into the contract! Part of her was impressed; the other part was just plain pissed off. Her dad was the most prolific and creative dealmaker in history, and here she was, still dicking around with a simple purchase contract. If her dad could convince people to barter away their eternal souls, she should be able to convince a reluctant heir to sell his stake in a failing family business, damn it!

Damien sat in his leather chair and took a sip of

his whiskey. "Why is this Daniel Webster suddenly coming out of the woodwork to challenge the sale? We've been negotiating with these folks for two months..."

Devlin shook her head and threw up her hands. "I honestly have no idea. In all of the facility tours, negotiations, and meet-and-greets, his name never came up. Everybody seemed on board with the sale. The money was worth more to them than trying to resuscitate the business." She sighed and rubbed her temples. "I'll be making an appointment to sit down with Mr. Webster to find out exactly what he's really after."

Damien tossed the contract onto the coffee table and winked at his daughter. "I know you'll get to the bottom of this and seal the deal. My girl is capable of anything!" He suddenly became serious. "Just make sure he understands that if he doesn't come around to seeing reason, we'll eviscerate him...in court of course." He smiled like a shark.

"Of course." Devlin chuckled and rolled her eyes. *Yup, being the human daughter of the Devil sure has its weird moments,* she thought. "I'll be giving Mr. Webster a call tomorrow to set up an appointment. I'll try to get this done civilly. No need to start off with threats."

"Sadly," Damien replied as he set his snifter down on the table. "I'll be gone for a week or so, and knowing you, you'll have this whole mess cleaned up by the time I get back."

"Business trip?" Devlin asked.

"I have to head to Hell for a check-in. It's been a few years, and despite his many natural talents, Mephistopheles is still a poor substitute for the real thing," Damien said, tweaking his sparkling diamond cufflinks. A dinner at home was still no excuse to be shabbily dressed.

Devlin chuckled. "So modest, as always!"

"How many times do I need to tell you, my girl, that modesty is for ordinary people, and you and I are anything *but* ordinary," Damien joked, raising an eyebrow. "But on a serious note, you truly are extraordinary, Devlin, and not just because you're my kid." He smiled tenderly at her and reached over to squeeze her hand. "Now, you're going to have to let your old man start packing for this trip. Keep me updated on the contract negotiations. The signal isn't great back home, but I may be able to pick up a message here and there."

Devlin smiled at her dad tenderly. She wouldn't trade him for the world, devil or not. "Will do, Dad. Have a good trip, and I'll keep you posted." She'd have her assistant look into Daniel Webster. There had to be *something* she could use to persuade him to sign the contract. After all, everyone had a price.

CHAPTER THREE

Devlin took a sip of her takeaway cappuccino and sighed. *Perfection!* Today was going to be a good day. She'd get her assistant to make an appointment with Daniel Webster, do some background on him, and come up with a plan to tackle his objections to the sale of Harvest Time Garden Market. She smiled to herself as the elevator dinged and the stainless-steel doors slid open. Devlin stepped out and glided past the reception desk, her Jimmy Choos clicking on the marble tile. She was so lost in her thoughts mapping out how she was going to tackle her day, that it took her a moment to register the panicked sounds of her assistant trailing her down the hall. Devlin turned to face Kitty, her assistant of five years, as she screeched to a halt in front of her.

"Someone named Daniel Webster is here for you. He wouldn't wait in the lobby. He just marched on through to the offices! I'm so sorry. I couldn't stop him!" Kitty said with her eyes wide in distress. "I tried to get him to book an appointment for later in the week, but he flat-out refused and said that come hell or high water he'd be meeting with you today!"

Devlin reached out and squeezed Kitty's arm reassuringly. "It's okay. I'll handle it."

"I know I just hate that you're walking into this first thing in the morning. It's so unprofessional!" Kitty said, anxiously wringing her hands.

"It's fine. I was going to book a meeting with him later this week anyhow. It just seems like that'll be happening a bit sooner than expected." Devlin took a couple of steps toward her office before doing a half-turn back to Kitty. "While I'm dealing with Mr. Webster, can you do me a favor?"

"Of course! Anything!" Kitty exclaimed, looking relieved to be done with the unwanted visitor currently squatting in her boss's office.

"I need you to do some digging. I need to know as much as I can about Daniel Webster. Look at everything, business dealings, personal life...whatever you think I can use as leverage to get him on board with the sale of his family's business."

Kitty smiled conspiratorially. "Anything for you, boss-lady!"

Devlin was back off down the hallway with a wink and a wave. There had been no sense in showing her annoyance to Kitty. That would just have served to upset her...but *what the hell?* she thought. *What kind of douchebag just shows up and barges their way into someone's office uninvited?* Between the red-lines on the contract and this insanely rude impromptu meeting, Daniel Webster was already getting on her nerves. *Who does this guy think he is?*

As she approached, she saw the back of a tall man with chestnut-brown hair and a crisp white shirt through the floor-to-ceiling glass wall of her office. He was examining her collection of trophies from Law Society award ceremonies that were lined up on a shelf like little soldiers. He'd taken off his jacket and slung it across the back of one of her chairs, his laptop bag was on the floor, and the laptop open on her desk. He'd clearly been using her office as a temporary workspace while he waited. *The nerve.* Devlin narrowed her eyes at his back as she entered the room. Her blood was beginning to boil.

"You must be Mr. Webster," Devlin announced, causing her uninvited guest to spin around awkwardly. Turning to hang her coat on the rack near the door, she indulged in a self-satisfied smile at his stumble. Like her dad always reminded her, it was important to get the upper hand early. With any luck, she'd manage to set him back on his heels a bit, and he deserved no less for showing up out of the blue. Despite her annoyance, she couldn't help but admit that, while he may be rude, he *was* easy on the eyes. Speaking of eyes, his hazel ones passed over her in a quick up-and-down, sizing her up.

"Uh, yes, Daniel Webster," he said as he cleared his throat, adjusted his glasses, and tugged on his loosely knotted tie. "You must be Devlin Laflamme," he said, his voice suddenly turning to steel.

Devlin raised an eyebrow at the change. Perhaps he wouldn't be so easy to throw off-kilter after all. "Well, that *is* the name on the outside of the door if I'm not mistaken," she replied snarkily. Devlin knew better, but this guy was getting under her skin. "I see you've made yourself at home." She motioned toward his belongings strewn around her office.

"Yes, well, I *have* been waiting a while," he replied, forgoing the traditional "first meeting" handshake to sit in the chair he'd commandeered in front of her desk.

Devlin shook her head in disbelief as she made her way to her own chair and sat. "You could have avoided the wait by making an appointment with my assistant. I was going to reach out to you today to go over the sale contract—"

Daniel cut her off mid-sentence. "There won't be a contract to go over. We're not selling."

Devlin's eyebrows crawled right up her forehead as she took in his pronouncement. "I'm afraid the other heirs to the business seem to be of a different opinion. We've had a verbal agreement for a couple of weeks now, the contract has been negotiated, and the only thing left to do is sign on the dotted line." She placed her laptop on the desk in front of her and powered it on. "I was going to do you the courtesy of booking a meeting to talk about additional considerations, given your obvious reluctance to sell, as evidenced by the copious notes you so generously provided, but you don't have the ability to stop the sale by yourself...not when the other heirs are in favor of the terms."

Daniel narrowed his eyes on her. "*You* were going to do *me* the courtesy of booking a meeting?"

"I know it may be a concept that is lost on you given how *you've* just shown up at *my* office with no warning, but yes," Devlin replied.

"You corporate fat-cat attorneys are all the same, out to tear apart the little guy for your own profit, no matter the cost. You're the spawn of Satan, all of you!" Daniel spat out.

"You have no idea," Devlin muttered under her breath.

"If you had an ounce of courtesy, you would have made sure *all* the heirs were on board before starting to negotiate a purchase. That's just the *right* thing to do, but I wouldn't expect someone like *you* to care about the right thing."

Devlin had officially had enough of this guy. "Right, an evil attorney like me... Well, let me clarify something for you, Mr. Webster. I have no legal responsibility to start tracking down every heir before negotiating a purchase. We had a majority that were interested in selling their stake in the business." She got up and moved toward the door of her office. "Furthermore, the sale has been in progress for weeks now, so where have you been all this time? Maybe you should have had a chat with the rest of your family before barging into my office to accuse me of having no moral compass." Devlin motioned to the exit. "At this time I'd like to invite you to leave. Any further communication can go through my assistant."

Daniel sat there for a minute, opening and closing his mouth like a fish. Devlin was tempted to laugh despite her anger. What a douche-canoe! He finally got control of himself and tossed his laptop in its bag, slinging it over his shoulder with enough force that Devlin heard it slap him in the ass. *And what an ass,* she thought, before mentally facepalming herself for being an idiot. *Note to self, do not ogle the enemy!* He grabbed his coat and marched over to where she stood at the door and stopped, staring her down like he was working up a snappy come-back. It never materialized. With a shake of his head, he stormed out the door and down the hall toward the elevators.

Good riddance, Devlin thought as she watched him disappear from sight. The last thing she needed during a tough negotiation was to be side-tracked lusting for opposing counsel. Heading back to her desk, she plopped back down with a sigh. *Why are the hot ones always such dicks?* So much for an easy resolution to this one. She was looking forward to seeing what Kitty had unearthed about Daniel Webster.

CHAPTER FOUR

Devlin sighed in bliss as she curled up on her couch at the end of another long-ass day. There was nothing quite like some quality couch time in her pajamas with a glass of wine and a good book. Tonight, there was going to be a slight modification. Instead of a book, Devlin pulled out her laptop and powered it on, letting it rest in her lap as she reached over to pick up her glass of pinot noir. It was time to get cracking on the file Kitty had sent her. She'd spent the whole day digging into every aspect of Daniel Webster's life. With any luck Devlin would find her silver bullet somewhere in the *Douche-Nozzle Dossier,* as they were calling it. There was no way in hell this deal wasn't going to be closed by the time her dad got back from his trip *to* Hell. Daniel had better hold on to his hat!

Devlin took a sip of wine and smiled to herself as she opened the file. Setting her wine glass on the coffee table, Devlin got down to business. She opened the sub-folder labeled *Family.* The Webster family tree popped up on her screen. There he was, Daniel Webster, the eldest son of George Webster, late owner of Harvest Time

Garden Market. That probably explained why he felt like he had some sort of extra-special power to negate the sale, but legally, his share was worth no more and no less than his siblings'. He had four siblings, two brothers and two sisters, who Devlin had the privilege of meeting during the course of negotiations. A couple of them had made half-assed attempts to run the business after their father's death, but their appalling lack of business acumen had led to near-catastrophic revenue losses in a very short time span. The other siblings seemed to have a visceral aversion to work in general, having spent their entire adult lives mooching off their father's estate. The consensus among Daniel's siblings had been to take the money from the sale of the Harvest Time grocery chain and run. Maybe Daniel had some sort of deep-seated desire to fuck with his siblings that would become clear as she dug into the rest of his life.

She took another sip of wine and opened the folder labeled *Career and Education*. There was a copy of his transcript from the University of Toronto Faculty of Law. *Very nice*, Devlin thought. She'd been accepted there herself but had ultimately chosen to attend Osgoode Hall instead. He was obviously a smart guy based on his grades. He'd definitely graduated at the top of his class with marks like that! She flipped to the document that listed his work history. It looked like he'd spent his career practicing family law, primarily adoption and child protection. He specialized in a very different aspect of the law than she did, but that didn't explain his nasty comments about corporate lawyers!

Shaking her head, Devlin closed that folder and moved on to the one marked *Social Media*. This was the stuff she was *really* looking forward to digging into! Mr. Webster seemed to have a *very* active life on social media. There were the requisite Facebook posts and Instagram snaps showing a smiling Daniel dining at chic restaurants, partying at fancy clubs, chilling in a well-appointed condo, and lounging on the dock at a *very* posh-looking cottage. Devlin rolled her eyes. Almost any one of these photos could have been printed in some glossy lifestyle magazine.

His siblings were in some of the photos, showing off their fancy cars and accessories. Every single photo featured a stunningly gorgeous brunette draped across Daniel's lap, kissing his cheek, or lounging against his chest. The glasses must be part of his Clark Kent persona for meetings; these photos were all Superman. Funny, but she was partial to the glasses.

Devlin eyed her wine glass and shook her head. She really needed to slow down on the booze if she wanted to nurse a healthy dislike of this man! Maybe it was time to switch out her morning affirmations from "you are worthy" to "Daniel is an offensively impolite jerk."

He looked like he had the picture-perfect life, so why was he so angry, and why hadn't he gotten involved in the early stages of the sale negotiations? She had to be missing something. Devlin blew out a frustrated breath and started going through the folder again from scratch, paying closer attention to what *wasn't* in the pictures. As she flipped through them slowly, Devlin noticed something she hadn't seen before. Every photo was at least five years old. There was a complete absence of anything since, as though Daniel Webster had ceased to exist.

Devlin set her laptop down and exchanged it for her wine. She made a decision as she swirled the ruby liquid around in her glass. There was a story here that she needed to get to the bottom of, or there wouldn't be a hope in hell of understanding Daniel Webster. It was time to take a field trip to North Bay, the home of Harvest Time Garden Market *and* Daniel Webster. If there were answers to be had, Devlin was convinced she'd find them there. Once she found out what made him tick, closing this deal would be like shooting fish in a barrel.

CHAPTER FIVE

What on Earth made me think a road trip to North Bay in February is a good plan! Grrr. Devlin growled and cursed as she drove hunched over the steering wheel of her rental car, peering through the driving snow like a grandma. She'd been driving for hours, but the blizzard had only started about thirty minutes ago, and it looked like it had no intention of letting up any time soon. *Why did I not ask for snow tires? City girls should not attempt winter driving outside of the Greater Toronto Area!* She felt the car slide a tiny bit to the left and her heart leapt into her mouth. Gripping the wheel tighter, she tried to put out good vibes that she'd manage to get to her hotel in one piece. Just as she had that thought, a clunking noise started under the hood.

"No no no no no, please!" Devlin begged as she felt her rental slow to a crawl. She had just enough forward momentum to pull off to the side of the highway as the vehicle gave up the ghost.

"Damn it!" she shouted and smacked the steering wheel. Devlin reluctantly threw the car into Park and

21

started digging around her purse to find her phone. It was at moments like this that she wished she'd allowed her dad to teach her the demonic summoning rituals that would have brought her help in mere seconds, but *noooo*, she'd wanted to live like a normal human and learn to solve her own problems. *Idiot!* What she wouldn't give to have a minion or two here to get her back on the road! She pulled her phone out of her bag and groaned as she realized she had no signal. *Come on!* Devlin threw her head back against the headrest and stared straight ahead. She had two choices. Stay in the car and slowly freeze to death, hoping that someone would stop to help her, or get out and try walking down the road until she got a signal on her phone. She looked at her coat in despair. It was definitely made more for fashion than function, and her boots with the little kitten heels were just as bad. The car would be as cold as the outdoors in no time, and she hadn't seen any other vehicles driving this stretch of highway in a while, so her best shot was to get out and walk.

Grumbling and promising to learn those damned rituals as soon as her dad got home, Devlin shrugged her arms into her woefully inadequate coat. This was gonna suck. She took a deep breath, threw open the car door, and squealed as the freezing cold wind whipped in and slapped her in the face. Her dad was the king of the fiery pits of Hell, and though she was human, she wasn't programmed for the cold either! *Mother fucker!* She slammed the door closed again and sat there in the driver's seat catching her breath and steeling herself for another exit attempt. *Now or never*, she thought as she opened the door and slid herself out into the blistering cold. She threw the door closed and shoved her thinly gloved hands under her armpits to try and keep them as warm as possible. She lasted about five steps before her little heels hit a patch of ice and she went sprawling across the soft shoulder of the highway, landing face-first in the snow.

Devlin dragged herself onto her butt as she shivered and sputtered, spitting snow out of her mouth and wiping it out of her eyes. As her vision cleared, she saw the most amazing sight she'd ever seen in her entire life—the red glow of taillights as a passing motorist stopped and began backing up to come to her rescue. *Praise the Dark Lord*, she thought as she dragged herself to her feet and began waving at her savior. She pasted on her brightest, most grateful smile as the car drew up next to her and the passenger window rolled down.

"You have no idea how thankful I am that someone was driving along this stretch of road! I haven't seen any other cars for ages…" She trailed off as she got her first view of the Good Samaritan who'd stopped to help her. The smile fell from her face, and he didn't look all that thrilled either. The Fates really were screwing with her today. Devlin was staring at a very annoyed-looking Daniel Webster.

CHAPTER SIX

One overweight suitcase, two near-faceplants, and a seriously vexed man draped in a laptop bag and a purse later, the car doors finally closed. Devlin felt like a human Popsicle, and she wasn't alone. She peeked over at Daniel, watching out the corner of her eye as he brushed piles of snow off his coat. It looked like he'd spent the day skiing Blue Mountain, and his anger was *definitely* piqued. The snow melting down her back didn't exactly make Devlin feel like a ray of sunshine either. The choice between freezing to death and being shut in a car with Daniel was a close race. She took a breath to steel herself and turned to look at her rescuer, determined to be gracious and thank him for the lift. *Be the change you wish to see in the world, and all that crap,* Devlin thought to herself. Daniel didn't even acknowledge her presence. He just kept staring straight ahead as he waited for the click of her seatbelt before pulling back out onto the highway. That was Devlin's first clue that this was *not* going to be like a trip to Disney. *Definitely not the happiest place on Earth. What a tool.*

They sat in the world's most awkward silence for what seemed like eternity. Devlin had a new suggestion for her dad if he ever decided to rework some torture scenarios. Refusing to put up with another second of this nonsense, Devlin turned to face Daniel, and as the Fates would have it, they both piped up at once.

"Thank you for the ride."

"What are you doing up here?"

There was a strange dance of hand flapping as they each gestured for the other to speak first. "Please, I insist," Devlin said aloud, hoping they could move past this horrifying awkwardness.

Daniel took a deep breath and nodded. "What are you doing in this neck of the woods?"

Shit, Devlin thought. She was hoping to avoid running into Daniel directly until she had armed herself with some useful information, but it looked like she was going to have to come clean...ish. She shot a glance at Daniel, crossed her fingers, and was about to speak when he shifted slightly toward her. Their eyes met and locked. It must have only been a few seconds, but Devlin felt her breath catch and her heart speed up. He was looking at her with an intensity she had never felt before. She swallowed hard as he broke eye contact to turn his focus back to the road, his hands tightening on the steering wheel enough to make the leather of his winter driving gloves creak.

"Um, yeah." She was flustered in a very out-of-character way. *Girl, calm yourself!* "After our meeting I figured it would be best to come to North Bay in person for a site visit. I was hoping we could sit down and hash out the best way forward for everyone involved." She sneaked a peek at Daniel's profile. His jaw was clenched, and his eyes stayed fixed straight ahead. Devlin gave him a moment to speak, and when he didn't, she forged on. "I know you're playing catch-up on this deal, and your reasons are your own, but we've worked very hard for this sale to benefit all parties."

Daniel barked out a derisive laugh. "What could you possibly know about hard work? You're an attorney at your father's corporation. Human resources probably got a memo the minute you finished law school instructing them to hire you." He laughed and shook his head before continuing. "I may be from North Bay, but I've spent enough time in Toronto on business to have seen how often you're featured in the lifestyle magazines and the who's-who gossip rags. Daddy's little princess. I hope that silver spoon wasn't too much of a burden."

"Excuse me?" Devlin tried to interject, but Daniel was on a roll.

"Of all the things you could be doing with your time, becoming a soulless corporate vampire sucking the life out of family legacies is what you chose." He shook his head and snorted in disgust.

There was no way in hell she was going to sit and listen to this bullshit for one more moment. Daniel was going down! "Let me stop you right there," Devlin said as she narrowed her eyes at him. "You don't know the first thing about me. How dare you presume to have any idea what my life has been like and what my motivations are." Devlin felt her blood pressure rising. "I was being generous before, but if you had such a strong opinion about the fate of your family's business, then why have you been MIA throughout this whole negotiation? Don't talk to me about caring about legacies. It obviously meant precious little to you until very recently." *Mic drop,* she thought with satisfaction.

Devlin swore Daniel looked like he'd been slapped, but the moment passed too quickly for her to be sure. His face went cold and stony. "You can do whatever you like on your site visit, but if you think I'm going to make it easy for you, you're delusional."

Devlin's blood was speeding through her veins like a runaway bullet train, and her head felt like it was about to explode. "Contrary to popular opinion, I don't go out of my way to ruin your day when I wake up in the morning," she spat out, her voice laced with contempt. "Quite frankly, you're the last thing on my mind, and I prefer life that way."

She raised a hand to rub her aching temple. *Perfect timing for a migraine.* As Devlin mentally lamented her shitty decision to visit North Bay, the car radio clicked on of its own accord and started rapidly changing stations. Daniel was cursing and fumbling with the dials, trying to shut the damn thing off, but it wouldn't play ball. Devlin retreated into her thoughts as her head pounded. The sounds in the car became muted and faded into the distance. She stared out the window at the driving snow as it barreled toward the windshield. Under its hypnotic effect, her breathing slowed, and the pounding in her head eased off. She took one last calming breath as her brain seemed to reconnect with her body. The car was quiet; the radio was off. Daniel had gone back to staring straight ahead, his profile cold and closed off. Devlin let her head drop back onto the headrest. She couldn't wait to get to her hotel to wash this day off of her. She must be reeking of anger and bad life choices.

CHAPTER SEVEN

An hour later, a *very* drained Devlin dragged her sorry ass into her room and kicked the door shut behind her. She had never been so happy to see a hotel in her entire life! The feeling must have been mutual if Daniel's car peeling out of the car park was any indication.

She dropped her purse onto the carpeted floor with a soft thud, walked across the room, and collapsed onto the bed, feeling like she'd just come off a battlefield. Devlin had never met anyone in her entire life that infuriated her quite like Daniel Webster. He was the most aggravating man she'd ever met, and something about his ability to argue a point well enough to challenge her made him freakin' hot, which disturbed her to no end! She was sweating bullets, and her neck and face were flushed, as though she'd just sprinted a mile in her favorite Manolos. Devlin rarely let anything fluster her, but her exasperation with Daniel was cooking her from the inside out!

With a groan, Devlin wriggled out of her jacket and tossed it onto the chair in the corner of the room.

She flopped onto her side and eyed the suitcase sitting next to the door. *Just get it done.* Sighing, Devlin pushed herself back upright and shuffled over to her bag. *How awesome would it be to throw an epic tantrum like a toddler right now?* She shook her head in a less than effective attempt to throw off the annoyances of the day and hauled her bag over to the bed.

With what felt like the last dregs of strength left in her body, she hefted her suitcase up, yanked the zipper around, and flipped the top open. The concierge had managed to make arrangements for a tow truck to head down the highway and rescue her rental car. The local garage would be able to take a look at it in the morning. In the meantime, Devlin wanted nothing more than to wash this day off her. She dug around in her bag and grabbed her favorite shampoo and body wash. If the only silver lining of the day was smelling good, she'd take it for a win at this point.

With a smile of anticipation, Devlin headed into the bathroom. *Yup, the day is starting to look up.* Her smile got only bigger as she twisted the faucet and heard the calming drum of water hitting the tile. She peeled off her clothes as a warm haze filled the room, letting them drop to the floor at her feet. Steam clung to her skin and made her shiver as the cold air of the bedroom snaked over her; goosebumps covered her arms as she slid into the welcoming warmth of the shower stall.

Devlin popped the top off her body wash and squeezed a healthy dollop into the palm of her hand. She breathed in the scent of vanilla as she ran a soapy hand across her stomach. Rivulets of suds left tingling trails down her body. *Maybe it would help to let off a little steam...* Devlin slipped one hand between her legs, as the other slid up her abdomen to close around her breast, her thumb moving back and forth across her nipple. She began to flip through the mental slideshow of her go-to spank-worthy hotties, but every single one of them seemed to have a giant Daniel Webster head that glared at her with disdain. Devlin tried to shake it off, but he was talking now, and that was the kiss of death.

"You have no sense of history and zero respect for a lifetime's work. You couldn't even fathom what this business means to communities around the province," he said, loathing dripping from every word.

Devlin leaned her forehead against the cool tile as her hands fell away from her body. That was worse than having a bucket of ice water dumped over her head. It really was a shame that such a hot man was such a massive douche waffle!

She made quick work of the rest of her shower, lest the specter of Daniel should make a return visit. Devlin wrapped herself in a towel and stepped out onto the bath mat. She was thoroughly done with this day and just wanted to sleep it off. She grabbed a facecloth and wiped at the steamed-up mirror. A scream caught in her throat as she met her own gaze. Panic rose inside her as she stared at blood-red eyes swimming with glowing embers. She spun away from her reflection and desperately sucked in air in a bid to stop her head from spinning. After a few deep breaths, she slowly turned, clutching the porcelain sink for dear life and staring into the drain to avoid catching a glimpse of herself in any reflective surface. She steeled herself and blinked hard then raised her head to defiantly stare herself down.

Nervous laughter bubbled up and out of her. *I must be two tacos short of a combo.* She stared into her perfectly normal green eyes with relief. *That's what you get for burning the candle at both ends.* She made a mental note to ease off on the caffeine and vowed to get eight hours of sleep tonight. Devlin rolled her eyes at herself in the mirror and headed to bed. She'd need a good night's sleep if she was going to go another twelve rounds with Daniel again tomorrow.

CHAPTER EIGHT

Devlin had spent half the night lying awake replaying the car ride from hell in her mind. She mentally kicked herself every time she thought up a better comeback than she'd used in the moment. She was so tired her eyebags had eyebags. Determined not to look as tired as she felt, Devlin had done some of the best concealer work she'd ever applied. *Thank you, YouTube tutorials,* she thought with a wry smile. She'd be fine once she got some caffeine into her. *Maybe an IV drip of espresso?*

Devlin eyed her flimsy coat with trepidation. She'd had the good sense to pack pants, but the coat was nowhere near warm enough. Bundling up as best she could, Devlin made an executive decision that her first mission of the day would be to buy more appropriate outerwear. Coffee wouldn't do her much good if she died of hypothermia first! She threw on her coat, slung her purse over her shoulder, and steeled herself to face the day. Come hell or high water, this sleuthing trip was going to be a game changer; she just had a gut feeling. *Or maybe that's just hunger...nah...*

Thankfully Devlin's hotel was on a busy street with lots of stores and plenty of cafés to hit for her caffeine fix. She walked *very* gingerly in her kitten-heeled boots. The sidewalk had been well salted, and she was terrified of stepping on a chunk and rolling an ankle. Nobody needed *that* in their life! A mannequin wearing a long red winter jacket caught her peripheral vision as she teetered along with her eyes glued to the pavement. Red. *Yasss! Be still my beating heart.* Devlin moved faster than she had all morning, scooting into the store and breathing a sigh of relief at the warmth as the door closed firmly behind her. The tinkling of the little bell above the door was the most beautiful sound in the world. A little retail therapy was occasionally good for the soul.

The red coat was calling her name. She walked over to the window display to get a closer look. As she flipped over the tag to read the size, Devlin heard someone approach.

A well-practiced customer service voice floated in from behind her. "Can I help you with anything?"

"Yes, please." Devlin turned to face a brightly smiling woman with way too much makeup, massive chunky earrings…and necklaces…and bracelets…and rings. She really should have taken some of Coco Chanel's advice and removed one accessory. "I'd like to know if you have this coat in other sizes…" Devlin trailed off as she watched the saleswoman's face turn to thunder.

"We don't have anything for you here." The woman flipped her hair with all the flair of a high school mean girl to reveal a name tag that read Brenda.

"Pardon?" Devlin asked as her eyes moved from Brenda to scan the rest of the store for another more helpful salesperson.

Brenda's superior look ratcheted up a notch as she gave Devlin an extremely catty once-over. "Yeah, nobody in town will have anything in your size, so there's really no point in wasting your time." Brenda moved toward the door and wrenched it open, motioning for Devlin to exit. "You have yourself a *super fantastic* day." The sarcasm dripping from her voice could have filled up Lake Nipissing.

"Okay," Devlin muttered as she held her hands up in surrender and walked back through the open door into the freezing cold February weather. *Well, she was spicy! What the fuck???*

Devlin stood in the biting cold completely gobsmacked by what had just happened. If that was how Brenda treated out-of-town customers, her Google reviews must suck! Taking a deep breath, Devlin headed down the sidewalk looking for the next clothing store. At this point she couldn't care less if the coat was red or fluorescent green, so long as it was warm! As she walked, the weirdest thing kept happening. As she approached each store, a salesperson would flip the "open" sign to "closed." Devlin yanked at the cuff of her coat to peer at her watch. It wasn't even ten in the morning. There was no way shops were closing for lunch this early. Whatever fresh hell *this* was, it exponentially increased her need for coffee. *A liquid hug for the brain!*

As though the universe had finally decided to smile on her, there was a quaint-looking café right across the street. Devlin flew as fast as her little heels could carry her, her fingers crossing as she approached the door, waiting for a "closed" sign to materialize in front of her. She held her breath as she peeked through the window at a lady in an apron behind the cash register, her hand reaching out toward the door handle slowly, signaling her intent to enter. At that moment the most beautiful thing happened. The woman looked directly at Devlin, smiled, and waved her in.

Devlin sighed in relief; her thoughts had already drifted to what she wanted to order. It felt like the world had gone crazy and all she could do was operate on caffeine and cynicism.

"You must be the lawyer from Toronto," the woman behind the counter pronounced as she gave Devlin a pitying look.

"Is it that obvious?" Devlin's eyebrow raised in question.

"Diane," the woman said as she extended her

hand in greeting.

Devlin was incredulous as she reached out to shake Diane's hand. "This is a far cry from the reception I seem to be getting everywhere else I've been today!"

"Why don't we have a chat. Take a seat, hon," Diane said, motioning toward a small, round, two-seater table. "What can I get you?"

"A cappuccino would be great, thank you." Devlin slipped off her coat, slung it over the back of her chair, and sat down, grateful for the unexpected kindness.

"Coming right up!" Diane smiled and got to work.

Devlin watched her new favorite person as she buzzed about behind the counter, preparing what could only be described as liquid gold. Hopefully Diane would be able to explain why she felt like she was starring in an episode of *Punk'd*. Devlin wanted to kiss the fabulous woman as she delivered the goods and took a seat across the table.

Devlin lifted the cup and inhaled deeply, drawing life from the aroma of coffee. It felt like a balm to her injured pride, soul, feelings, sanity… *Pick a card, any card.* She took a small sip of the piping-hot drink and sighed in pleasure. "This has to be the best cappuccino I've ever tasted." She smiled at Diane with pure gratitude. "Thank you."

"You're welcome." Diane chuckled. "I figured

you'd need something warm after the cold shoulder you got on your way here. I was watching from the window."

Devlin snorted. "I don't think I've *ever* inspired that level of hatred before! Something new to put on the resume."

Diane sighed. "You certainly didn't deserve that kind of treatment, but I can give you a bit of context."

"I'd love nothing more," Devlin said with gratitude.

Diane nodded and began. "Daniel and his siblings all grew up here. Everybody has known them since they were children. My son played with Daniel when they were in kindergarten. They were friends until Daniel left to go to Toronto for university." Diane smiled at the memories. "Harvest Time Garden Market was a labor of love for their father, George. He started a small farm-to-table grocery store and grew the business from the ground up. He wanted every customer to feel like they were part of the family, and it wasn't just lip service. George had the whole family involved in volunteer work in the community. They built the corporate office here in North Bay instead of relocating to Toronto. They donated a lot of money to local charities and community groups. George was a fixture in the area. It was a huge loss for all of us when he passed away."

"So, everyone's giving me the brush-off because my company is buying the business and it's part of Mr.

Webster's legacy." Devlin sighed. "That makes sense. Daniel talked a lot about community on the car ride here. I just didn't realize how much the business meant."

Diane smiled at her sadly. "There's more to this story." She wiped at a water mark on the counter. "You have to understand that Daniel has always been loved and respected here. When his siblings wanted to party at the lake house, he was working in the stock room at one of his father's stores. When his brothers were getting into trouble, he was helping out at charity events. The community doesn't want to see him hurt. Since he's been back, all he's spoken about or cared about is stopping the sale of the business to protect his family's legacy...his *father's* legacy..." Diane trailed off.

"I see." Devlin nodded, turning the information over in her head. "I'm not here to hurt Daniel, or the community, but there's a legal sale process that's running its course, and there really isn't anything that can be done at this point. But it helps to know a bit more about where he's coming from. I really appreciate it, Diane." Devlin sat back and sipped her cappuccino. She was determined to make a concerted effort to soften her approach with Daniel. There were still a lot of question marks, like why was he just popping up now, but regardless of where he'd been during the negotiation, the business clearly meant a great deal to him. Devlin resolved to be more compassionate. *Look at that,* she thought, *personal growth…#winning!*

CHAPTER NINE

Devlin left the café with a quick wave to Diane. She had bounce to her step as she met the arriving Uber. She'd learned a lot from Diane in the half-hour they'd spent together, and it felt really good to have someone that was willing to give her the benefit of the doubt. Armed with a bit more context on *why* the business was so important to Daniel, Devlin hoped that she'd be able to wave the white flag and call for parlay.

She pulled out her phone and shot a quick text to Kitty, letting her know that she was on her way to the Harvest Time head office and that she'd be unreachable for most of the day. The trip to the office was only about ten minutes, but it gave Devlin time to formulate a plan of attack. Unlike Daniel's performance at her office, Devlin would have a nice chat with reception. Hopefully she could tease some information out of the receptionist about Daniel's state of mind. With any luck, they'd spill the beans on how his sudden intrusion into the sale had been received by his siblings. The Uber pulled up at her destination. With a smile to the driver, she got out and headed into the belly of the beast.

To be fair, the beast was pretty well decorated. Devlin looked over the clean, modern decor with an approving eye. It was a two-story building with glass-walled meeting rooms and floor-to-ceiling windows that allowed the natural light to stream in. She would have expected to see happy employees buzzing around, going about their daily routines, but there was a vibe of fear and uncertainty despite the airy environment. Eyes locked on her with suspicion the moment she walked through the door. The receptionist's gaze shifted around as he tried to look anywhere *but* at Devlin as she approached the front desk.

"Hi." Devlin gave the receptionist her brightest smile.

He raised his eyes nervously. "Hello, welcome to Harvest Time Garden Market. How can I help you?" His voice wavered slightly.

Devlin noticed several employees in the vicinity creeping slightly closer in an effort to eavesdrop. As she turned to look at them, they scuttled away like bugs under a harsh light. Devlin turned back to the receptionist with a soft chuckle. "It seems like there's a bit of tension around here."

"That's the understatement of the year." He visibly relaxed and let out the breath he'd been holding. "You must be the lawyer...Ms. Laflamme? I'm Max."

He held out his hand to shake hers.

"Devlin." She smiled. She leaned in, whispering conspiratorially, "So, can you tell me a bit about what's been going on around here lately?"

Max glanced around to make sure nobody was listening. "This was always such a great place to work while Mr. Webster was alive. Since he passed away, it's been a nightmare."

Devlin raised an eyebrow and motioned for him to continue.

Max nodded. "Well, first of all, Jake and Chad took over and tried to run the business. I'm sure you've dealt with all of Mr. Webster's children at this point, so you know that they've never been particularly interested in operations. The business ran itself for a while. Once the money problems started, folks were quitting like rats leaving a sinking ship." He looked defeated.

Devlin nodded. "Yes, my firm was looped in on the financial challenges."

"Well, after the sale process started, the brothers basically disappeared. I haven't seen them in a couple of months." Max shrugged.

"And now?" Devlin asked.

Max pressed his lips and visibly tensed. "Mr. Daniel Webster has assumed the role of acting president since his return."

"And how have things been since Daniel has been

in charge?" Devlin frowned as Max seemed to shrink away before her eye at the mention of Daniel.

"I...I don't want to speak out of turn..." Max stuttered. "I've worked here for several years. Your company is buying the business. I don't want you to think I'm the sort of person who would badmouth my company president..." he trailed off.

Devlin gave him a reassuring smile. "I'd just like to get a feel for what to expect. That's all."

"Okay..." Max continued with trepidation. "Mr. Daniel Webster has been to the office every day. It's been...difficult for the staff. He seems angry with everyone and everything. It's been intimidating."

"I see," Devlin said, not the least bit surprised. *Sounds just like the Daniel I love to hate.*

"*You* didn't waste any time pushing in here." A familiar male voice, dripping with venom, echoed through the lobby.

Poor Max jumped a mile and scurried away with a stack of papers. Devlin hung onto her composure at Daniel's dramatic entry by the skin of her teeth. "So lovely to see you, Daniel," she said, pasting on a mask of professional cordiality. *Good adulting, Devlin, ten points to Gryffindor!* "I was hoping to meet with you today to discuss the contracts." The impulse to stick out her tongue at him raged within her.

Devlin gave Daniel a once-over, as she took in his

fashion choices. A far cry from the dress shirt and pants she'd seen him in before, he was wearing a pair of well-worn jeans and a fleece shirt. *Damn it, he looks just as good dressed down.*

"Well, that's not going to happen. I'm on my way to an off-site meeting." Daniel shrugged into a parka and zipped it up. "But," he said as he looked her up and down, "if you want to come with me, we can take our meeting on the road."

"Sounds like a plan," she said with a wary smile. *Danger, Will Robinson!* Something felt *very* off.

Daniel shot her the oddest look. "This should be fun." He aimed his keychain through the glass-paned door toward a company truck in the parking lot and hit the remote starter.

CHAPTER TEN

This is awkward, Devlin thought as they rumbled down the road in the truck. She was trying to figure out the best segue into the contracts when Daniel suddenly took an exit that led toward the highway.

"Where are we going?" she asked, whipping her head around to watch North Bay disappear behind them.

"You'll see." Daniel had a hint of amusement in his voice that made Devlin more nervous than she cared to admit.

"Super..." She tried to ignore the fact that there were cows and corn outside her window. Devlin cleared her throat. "About the sale contract..."

"Not now." Daniel cut her off and flipped the radio on. He started humming along with the country song filling the silence in the truck.

"If not now, then when?" Devlin muttered under her breath. *I'll take Annoying Men for $100, Alex.* Devlin sighed and resigned herself to watching farms slide by as she rested her forehead against the cool window. Daniel was just irritating enough to start her blood boiling, and

Devlin was not going to give him the satisfaction of seeing her sweat. *Calm blue ocean, calm blue ocean.* She was going to get this contract done come Hell or high water.

She was still reciting the mantra, which was *not* helping, as Daniel pulled the truck down an unpaved side road. *What the actual fu…*

"A farm?" she exclaimed as a barn came into view at the end of the long drive.

"A farm," Daniel confirmed as he looked at her with a smug smile. "I figured it would be good for you to see exactly what sort of business you were buying. You'll also get to see what you'll be destroying when you sell it off for parts." His disgust with her was clear as he pulled up in front of the barn and threw the truck into Park.

Daniel didn't give her a second glance as he set his glasses on the dashboard, opened his door, and hopped down. *What a tool.* Devlin sighed as she popped open her door and looked down at the muddy ground. This was one hundred percent on purpose. She slid down from the cab of the truck and felt the narrow heels of her boots sink into the mud. Thank all the legions of the Underworld that her experience with dirty boardroom tactics had taught her to control her face. *Here lies a perfectly good pair of Prada boots. They lived a good life and died heroes.* Devlin cringed as she eulogized her loss at the hands of Daniel the Dumbass.

Devlin picked her way as quickly as she could

across the soft ground, trying to catch up with Daniel, who was already at the door of the barn. He was chatting with an older man in well-worn denim overalls and gave her a mocking glance as he followed the man into the barn. *Oh no you don't, douchenozzle.* Devlin picked up her pace, reaching the men, who were deep in conversation, at lightning speed. She cleared her throat loudly, and Daniel turned toward her with a look of surprise at her sudden appearance.

"Uh, Joe, this is Devlin. She works for the company that's trying to buy Harvest Time." He motioned toward Joe. "Devlin, this is Joe. He's the owner of this farm and is one of our long-time local suppliers."

"Good to meet you." Devlin smiled as she shook Joe's outstretched hand. It was callused and strong, the hand of a man who did an honest, hard day's work.

Joe smiled at her as he released her hand, pointing down at her ruined boots. "I have a pair of my wife's rubber boots over there. Why don't you put those on, and I'll give you both a tour."

Devlin felt the warmth of pure, unadulterated gratitude course through her as she turned around, grabbed the *much* more practical rubber boots, and slipped them on, setting her ruined ones to the side. *Chivalry isn't dead after all.* She directed a scathing look toward Daniel, who lowered his gaze and kicked at some straw on the ground sheepishly. He looked like a schoolboy who'd just been scolded for sticking gum under his desk. Devlin *almost* laughed out loud but caught herself in the nick of time. There was no way she was going to have him thinking he was off the hook for being such a dick.

"What would you like to see?" Joe asked them both.

Daniel leaned forward and whispered something in his ear. Joe looked surprised as he responded, "Are you sure?" Daniel nodded and smiled.

"Follow me." Joe motioned for them to accompany him as they walked a short distance into a sterile area.

There were raised platforms on either side of the space with metal gates running the length of the room, ending at a set of hanging industrial refrigeration curtains. There were hoses and tubes everywhere, and it was giving a serious sci-fi vibe. *Beam me up, Scotty!* She turned to Daniel with a raised eyebrow as Joe disappeared through the curtains. He just smirked back at her, which did nothing to enhance her calm.

Cows suddenly streamed down both platforms. Joe came back in and headed over to a sink to wash his hands. Daniel motioned for Devlin to follow him. They stood side-by-side as they soaped up.

"Okay," Joe said as he walked to the nearest cow

with a spray bottle. "Time to sanitize the teats."

"I'm sorry. Time to *what?*" Devlin asked as Joe got to work rubbing the teats and udders. Her brain fuzzed out a bit as Joe talked about milk production and started showing her how to attach vacuums to the teats. *Ouch.*

"Why don't you give it a go?" Joe said, looking up at her from his crouched position.

"Oh, no…" she said, shaking her head, shuffling backward until she bumped into Daniel, who happened to be standing behind her. *Fuck.* She turned her head slightly and caught him looking a little too gleeful for her taste. She had just given him what he expected. *Well, screw you, sir!* "Sure, just walk me through it one more time," she said, smiling with false bravado. She made her way onto the platform, hoping against hope she wouldn't get kicked by a cow.

After another quick demo from Joe, Devlin got right in there, attaching the vacuum to the teats like a pro. Joe gave her an approving smile and motioned down the line of cows. She shot a smug smile at Daniel, who looked like he'd been slapped in the face. Devlin chuckled to herself as she started on the next cow. *Try harder next time, jackass.*

When all the cows had been fully milked and unhooked, they looked soothed and relaxed; they were clearly grateful to have their udders emptied! Devlin was feeling pretty satisfied with her work and was getting ready to wash her hands when more cows streamed onto the platforms.

"What the…" she muttered as she glanced from the cows to Joe in confusion. "How many cows do you have?"

Joe smiled. "About ninety more."

As if on cue, farmhands showed up to take over.

"Thank Hellfire," Devlin muttered with relief.

"Why don't we move on to the next part of the tour," Daniel said to Joe as he moved toward a side door, near the refrigeration curtains.

"Sounds like a plan." Joe motioned for Devlin to follow them.

They emerged into a massive space filled with huge pens of calves on both sides of a long alley. There was sawdust everywhere. Particles kicked up into the air and clung to her pants and coat as they walked the length of the structure toward a pair of large open doors. The smell of manure was overpowering her. Devlin had never wished for air freshener so hard in her life. *With any luck, I'll go nose blind soon.*

When they reached the open doors, Devlin stared in horror at a cavernous room full of small, square bales of hay. This wasn't going to end well.

"I need you to haul bales to the feed pens we passed so the calves can have their lunch." Joe shot an odd, questioning look at Daniel, who simply nodded and walked on through, peeling off his jacket and tossing it onto a bale of hay.

So, this is the plan, Devlin thought as she watched Daniel heft a bale into his arms and head past her toward the pens. *Well, buddy, I was born on a day, but not yesterday.* There was no way in Hell Devlin was going to let Daniel win this battle. If he wanted to make her uncomfortable, embarrass her, or make her seem weak, he had another think coming. She shrugged out of her coat, made a quick prayer of apology to the Burberry gods, and threw it onto the hay.

Devlin hauled bales as though her life depended on it. At one point Daniel took notice and picked up his pace. *What a baby.* She was not going to let him outdo her. Devlin matched Daniel, bale for bale, ignoring the blisters that were materializing on her palms. They were both dripping with sweat and covered in sawdust. Pieces of straw were stuck in her hair. This was no Paris Fashion Week!

"Good work!" Joe exclaimed. "You've both earned these." He tossed a bottle of water at each of them.

Devlin guzzled her water like she'd been wandering in the Sahara Desert for days. She pounded the whole bottle and wiped the dribbles of water off her chin with her sleeve. She felt Daniel's eyes on her and turned to give him a piece of her mind. He was giving her a weird look. Either it was respect, or he was having a stroke. Not quite sure what to make of it, Devlin just nodded awkwardly and turned back to Joe.

"What's next?" Devlin asked with a touch of challenge to her voice.

Joe smiled at her. "I think I have just the thing."

Devlin's mood shifted as they went into a cozy room off the milking parlor. In two small pens there were a dozen baby cows. They were the cutest things Devlin had ever seen. They looked up at her with their huge, innocent eyes, and her heart melted. Joe grabbed a couple of bottles of milk out of a refrigerator and passed them to Devlin and Daniel. They crouched down next to one of the pens side-by-side. Hungry babies immediately latched onto the nipples of the bottles and began sucking away happily. Devlin reached out to pet the impatient little beasts as they butted against each other in their desire to feed. She heard a chuckle beside her and turned to see Daniel watching her with a smile. Before she could stop herself, she smiled right back at him. *You're an idiot.* Figuring it would be better for her sanity, Devlin moved to the other pen. She wasn't about to ruin this experience worrying about Daniel Webster.

CHAPTER ELEVEN

Two hours later, Devlin emerged from the barn looking like a hot mess. She had changed out of her loaner boots and was picking dry mud off her heels as she waited for Daniel to say goodbye to Joe. She certainly hadn't expected to have *fun* today. *Better start keeping an eye open for flying pigs and a moon made of cheese.* Devlin was the quintessential city girl and had never pictured herself dodging cow shit and having a laugh about it! She smelled like a sewer, her clothes were a disaster, she had straw in her hair, and she couldn't have cared less. This was the most fun she'd had in a pretty long time, and she'd had fun in the vicinity of *Daniel* of all people.

She tried to sneak a covert look at Daniel, but as fate would have it, he chose that moment to shift his gaze over Joe's shoulder, and their eyes locked. *Balls!* Devlin hastily looked away as a blush crept over her cheeks. *Why did the giant dickwad suddenly decide to make himself less offensive?* She had seen a side of Daniel she hadn't known existed. If you'd asked her this morning, she would have thought a smile would make his face crack. Now she knew that he had a charming set of dimples and a slightly lopsided grin that gave him a bit of a roguish, up-to-no-good vibe. Joe clearly adored dealing with Daniel, and Daniel obviously had a good understanding of farming. This Daniel wasn't the absolute worst...

Devlin smiled and waved at Joe as Daniel turned toward her to leave. "Thank you so much for the tour. This has definitely been a memorable experience!"

"You're welcome back anytime." Joe smiled and winked before heading back into the barn.

"So, what did you think?" Daniel asked as they walked side-by-side to the truck.

Devlin looked up at him, searching his face for any sign of contempt or mocking. Nada. "When you said we were going to a meeting, this wasn't quite what I had in mind, but I actually kinda enjoyed it. Joe's a pretty great guy. It was good to see how a farm really works."

His eyebrows shot up in surprise, and that smile made another appearance. "Sometimes it's fun to get dirty."

Devlin choked on a laugh as her feet slipped out from under her in the slimy mud. Quick as a flash, Daniel's arms were around her, snatching her back from what would have been a *very* ugly landing. "Just not as dirty as *that* could have been," she joked as Daniel set her gently back on her feet.

"Yeah, you would have been *very* dirty," Daniel

said quietly, his arms still encircling her gently, holding her close enough that she could feel the soft whisper of his breath across her face as he spoke.

She felt like she was barely breathing. *It's overrated anyway.* Devlin raised her eyes to meet Daniel's. Those hazel eyes really were something, a dark green ring around the outside of his iris and a shifting kaleidoscope of honey-gold and blue. The blistering cold wind had zero effect on her in the warmth of Daniel's arms. The space between them seemed to shrink as though they were being drawn together by some kind of magic. Devlin felt lightheaded. Her world was pitching and shifting. *So, this is how Alice felt falling down the rabbit hole.* Their breath mingled as they drew ever closer. The tension mounted, and Daniel pulled her toward himself more firmly. *Is this really happening?* Devlin's thoughts were vague as she surrendered herself to the moment, tilting her face slightly to close the damnable space between their lips. And then her phone rang.

They sprang apart like scared rabbits. Devlin dug in her pocket to pull out her smartphone as Daniel shoved his hands into his pockets and nodded at her before loping off to the truck.

Devlin blew out a frustrated breath as she answered her phone. "Hello?"

"Devlin? Hi, it's Kitty. I'm so sorry to bother you. I just wanted to let you know that Chad Webster was following up this morning to see what the hold-up was on the sale. He's *very* eager to get his money."

"Thanks for letting me know, Kitty. Can you tell him that we're doing some final due-diligence and that I will get back to him as soon as it is complete?"

"Sure thing, boss! Sorry for bugging you," Kitty said with her characteristic high energy.

"Don't worry about it. My meeting was done anyhow. I'll keep you posted with any developments." Devlin sighed as she hung up the phone. Her body was buzzing. Poor Kitty had no idea how well-timed that call was. *Bad Devlin!* She glanced toward the truck. Daniel Webster looked *supremely* uncomfortable. She sighed. *Reality bites.*

CHAPTER TWELVE

Daniel drove her back to the hotel in silence. They had officially reached Awkwardness Level Expert! Devlin had practically launched herself out of the truck as he had pulled up in front of the hotel entrance.

She peeled off her clothes and jumped into a shower within a millisecond of walking through the door. She was desperate to wash off the stink and confusion of the day. The hot water was wonderful on her sore muscles. It felt like she'd gotten all of her workouts for the year in one shot. Despite her mental and physical exhaustion, Devlin's body was still humming from her near-miss with Daniel. Feeling a little guilty at her choice of inspiration, Devlin closed her eyes and gave in to the sensations skipping along her skin. She parted her lips in a sigh as she slid a soapy hand up to cup one of her breasts. As she rubbed her thumb across it, her nipple pearled and her body came alive. Her mind began to wander along with her hands...

A tall man facing away from her, chestnut hair brushing the collar of a crisp white shirt, his head slowly turning to reveal black framed glasses.

Devlin's breath hitched as her fingers left a tingling trail in their wake. Her fantasy man turned toward her; hazel eyes pierced her soul. Devlin's breathing came more rapidly as all the sensation in her body crystallized until she was on the edge of ecstasy. Her fantasy man stepped toward her, reaching out to pull her into his arms. Her body was flush against him, and his rock-hard cock rubbed against her as he rocked his hips back and forth gently.

Those hazel eyes bored into hers. One of his hands slid up into her hair, drawing her head toward his. Their lips touched, soft as a whisper. His tongue snaked out to lick along the seam of her lips, seeking entry. Devlin gasped. His tongue slid into her mouth, delving deep, exploring, twining with hers. His hand slid out from her hair and made its way down her body, slipping between her legs. His fingers moved deftly through her swollen folds, circling her entrance slowly and torturously before plunging into her depths.

Devlin cried out as her body bucked and clenched in waves. She reached out to brace herself against the tile wall of the shower as she caught her breath, still twitching. *Holy shit!* That had been one hell of a solo act. Now she had to find a way to look Daniel in the eye!

About half a dozen shampoos later, Devlin felt confident the smell of cow shit had been successfully vanquished. Time to get into her pajamas, sit the fuck down, order some room service, and do some work…or maybe crash for the day. Procrastination wasn't usually her thing, but today just might call for it, in addition to a very large glass of wine. Her hands were on fire from blisters, every muscle in her body was screaming, and she'd used up most of her body wash. Devlin looked mournfully at the garbage bags of clothes sitting on the floor near the door. Her Burberry top and coat were her favorite winter office clothes. Was there any hope of saving them, or was it time to plan their funerals? Either way, they couldn't stay inside. Her room was starting to smell like a barn.

With a sigh, Devlin picked up the phone and hit zero.

"Front desk, how can I help you?" The practiced customer service tone was just a touch too perky for Devlin's mood.

"Yes, hi." Devlin took a deep breath and reminded herself to behave like a grownup. "I'd like to make a room service order and to put in a request for dry cleaning."

"Fantastic! I can certainly help you with that today." The perkiness was unrelenting. "What would you like to order for your meal today?"

Would it be wrong to order a bottle of wine and leave it at that? Devlin sighed; sadly, alcohol alone didn't constitute a healthy meal. "I'll have a chicken Caesar salad and a glass of your house red."

"Excellent choice, Ms. Laflamme." Devlin heard a keyboard clicking over the line as her order was entered into the computer. "Your order should be at your door in about fifteen minutes. I'll have one of our porters pick up your dry cleaning. If you could leave the items in a bag outside of your room, someone will be there shortly. Is there anything else we can do for you this evening?"

"No, thank you, that's everything." Devlin hung up the phone and nipped over to her stinky bag of clothes. She was more than happy to get them the hell out of her room. She popped the door open and nudged the bag out into the hallway with her toe.

Devlin shut the door firmly behind her and took a deep, calming breath. *What a shitshow of a day!* She hadn't gotten *any* work done, and she had to catch up on *some* of it before she made a second attempt at contract revisions tomorrow. She pulled her laptop out and plopped down onto her bed to get comfy.

Devlin *really* had to email her dad. He'd be anxious to hear about her progress on the acquisition, not to mention a quick life update from his only daughter. The Wi-Fi signal in Hell was notoriously bad, so it was a crapshoot if he'd get the message, but she'd promised to update him, and she always kept her promises. She really had to get on her dad's case again about updating the infernal infrastructure and dragging Hell into *this* century! She'd heard through the stinging nettle that the trusted chancellors of many legions felt that administration was a real bitch. Management had to operate as though it were the Dark Ages! She'd never visited Hell herself of course. Mortals didn't exactly do well crossing the dimensional rift. They had an unfortunate tendency to tear apart at the molecular level. Since she'd never manifested any demonic traits, the assumption was that her human half had won the genetic battle. She'd live a normal mortal life. It wasn't like you could get a DNA test to double-check after all.

Devlin fired off a sufficiently vague email that would appease her dad, letting him know that she was performing a site visit. No need to alarm him with her lack of progress finalizing the contract. With that taken care of, she opened the file with the most recent version. As she scrolled through the document, Devlin realized that the red lines were starting to form a pattern. Each notation represented a frivolous amendment request designed to delay the sale of Harvest Time Garden Market. That time pushed the closing date suspiciously close to the date of the only "out" clause. How had she not seen this before?

It was a Hail Mary, but *if* revenues rose twenty-five percent before the closing date, the seller could back out and the deal would be canceled. It was a next-to-impossible feat given the sorry state of the company's finances, but it seemed Daniel was hoping for a miracle. Devlin pulled out her phone and texted Kitty, asking for the most recent financials for Harvest Time. If this was Daniel's plan, she really needed to sit him down for a reality check. Maybe if she went through some of the company records, she would be able to show him the futility of his endeavor. She sent Daniel a quick email requesting access to documentation and to book a meeting for the next day. *Let's rip the Band-Aid off quickly.*

At the knock on her door, Devlin closed her laptop. Her stomach growled like a Hellhound, and she realized she hadn't eaten anything all day. A porter carried a tray into the room and set it down on her nightstand. Devlin smiled and passed him a tip before he slipped out quietly. She sat on the edge of the bed and looked at her glass of wine. *Definitely not a large glass.* She pulled off the cellophane wrapped over the top of the glass to avoid spillage and took a big gulp. *May need to order another one of these for dessert.* She put the glass down and grabbed the handle of the tray cover that was hiding her salad. *Let's hope this chef likes to supersize their salads.* She lifted the lid and revealed a medium-sized salad. *Balls... Wine and a piece of cheesecake for dessert for sure.* She grabbed her fork and dug in, alternating between bites of chicken, lettuce, and sips of wine.

Devlin's mind wandered back to Joe's farm. She

had no idea how, but at some point, between punking her into dirty chores and catching her outside the barn, Daniel had briefly pulled the stick out of his ass. The way he'd been discussing pricing and volumes with Joe had taken her by surprise. He really knew the business, and he clearly had a good rapport with the local suppliers. It was obvious Daniel wasn't afraid of getting his hands dirty. He'd looked pretty hot hauling bales of hay, his arms flexing as he hoisted them up over the sides of the pens and wiping the sweat off his brow with the sleeve of his sweater.

I must be delusional, she thought as she put her fork down and stared at the empty wine glass on the bedside table. She'd come to North Bay to finish a business deal with a man she loathed. What the fuck was she doing sitting here lusting over him again? The shower fantasy should have been a one-and-done, but her thoughts focused with laser-like precision on the way his eyes had dilated as their lips had drawn closer. She was transported back to that moment, feeling the soft whisper of his breath as it feathered across her skin.

The sound of glass cracking jolted Devlin back to reality. The wine glass was splintered, long fissures spreading across and around it like spider webs. *What the fuck?* The hairs on the back of her neck stood on end as though she'd been hit with an electric charge. *Weird.* Devlin gently lifted the glass up by the stem and placed it back on the tray. She'd never seen anything like it. *It must be the changing temperature with the heater in the room kicking on and off.* She picked up the tray very carefully and moved it out onto the floor in the hallway next to her door. Devlin shook her head and rolled her shoulders, physically throwing off the odd vibe as she closed the door. Forget dessert, it was time to fall asleep streaming some bad reality TV.

CHAPTER THIRTEEN

Devlin smiled and waved at Max as she walked into the Harvest Time office the next morning. She'd left her pitchfork at home and was keeping her horns in. It was going to be a good day, damn it!

"Good morning, Max!"

To Devlin's surprise, Max seemed to pretend that he hadn't seen or heard her. He busied himself by shuffling papers around on his desk and "answering" a phone that hadn't rung. Devlin started wandering around the ground floor, trying to find someone who could direct her to a workspace. Since it seemed Max didn't want to give her the time of day, hopefully someone else would. Six failed-approach attempts later, Devlin was starting to wonder if she smelled bad or something.

Deciding to give up on finding a spare desk for now, Devlin went in search of coffee. She figured it would be best operating fully caffeinated to deal with whatever fresh fuckery was afoot. After a few minutes of wandering, she found a break room with a pod coffee machine. *Thank brimstone!* She hiked her laptop bag higher up on her shoulder as she started rifling through all the drawers and cabinets in a fruitless attempt at finding a stash of pods. *It's a two-story building. There has to be another break room upstairs.*

Her shoulder was going to have a perma-dent from the strap of her heavy bag, and it felt like an ice pick was boring into her brain from caffeine withdrawal. The level of suck was increasing, despite her valiant effort to think happy thoughts. The second floor was basically a ghost town. Devlin walked past empty offices, empty cubicles, and into an empty break room. There it was. The coffee machine sat on the counter, taunting her with possibility. She thought she had mentally prepared herself for disappointment, but the whimper of sadness when she came up empty in her search for pods yet again said otherwise. *What kind of cruel overlord deprives his staff of caffeine?* Even her dad kept the coffee flowing in the unhallowed halls of the administration buildings in Limbo.

With a heavy heart, Devlin headed back into the office area, on the search for someone, *anyone*, who could find her a desk. It looked like the zombie apocalypse had rolled through Harvest Time. Piles of work were laid out on desks, pens looked like they had been dropped in an instant, coffee cups that were half-full sat cooling... *Wait...coffee cups?* Devlin's eyes narrowed as she zeroed in on one cup that still had a touch of steam rising from the liquid inside. *Fuckery indeed.*

As Devlin walked back to the stairs, she heard a toilet flush and realized she was passing a washroom. It was now or never. She flung open the door and strode in, surprising the crap out of the person washing their hands at the sink.

"Hi, I'm Devlin," she said with a big fake smile, extending her hand.

"Uh, Adrian," they replied, grabbing a paper towel and drying their hands quickly to shake Devlin's hand.

"Good to meet you, Adrian." Devlin felt bad for cornering them, but she was at her wits' end. "I was hoping you could help me. I'm supposed to be meeting with Daniel Webster today, and I need to find a place to work until then...and some coffee."

Adrian looked oddly nervous. "I...um...It's just..."

Yup, definite fuckery, and it was Daniel-shaped. "It's okay. I'm guessing the staff has been instructed to be less than helpful today?"

Adrian nodded. "Yeah, sorry... Listen, I'd love to help you with the coffee thing..." They leaned in toward Devlin and whispered, "Mr. Webster had all of the coffee pods packed into a box that he has stashed in his office. I'll go in and grab you one when he comes out."

Devlin stuffed down the impulse to shout *I knew it* at the top of her lungs. "Thank you so much." She smiled as she replied. "Do you know who I should see about a work space? Max seemed to be otherwise occupied when I arrived."

"Hmmm." Adrian took a moment before responding. "You know what, this whole thing is ridiculous. Come downstairs with me and I'll talk to Max and see if he can get you a desk."

"You are officially my favorite person today!" Devlin could have hugged Adrian for being a fantastic human.

Adrian poked their head out of the washroom, looking up and down the hallway furtively before stepping out and motioning for Devlin to follow. It felt like the *Mission Impossible* theme should have been playing as they slunk down the stairs and back into the lobby.

Max gave Adrian an exasperated look as they approached the front desk. "What are you doing?" he asked them in a stage whisper.

"Come on." Adrian rolled their eyes. "You can't feel good about letting her just wander around, Max."

He looked appropriately contrite as he replied, "You're right. I'm sorry, Devlin. I just didn't want to be the one to…" Max looked distressed. "Follow me." He sighed as he got up and came around the front desk.

Instead of heading toward the part of the office filled with desks and cubicles, they went across the lobby to a door that was hidden behind the staircase. Devlin was starting to get Harry Potter vibes, and was pretty sure no good could come of this. The situation didn't improve when Max gave her an apologetic look and opened the door.

Qu'est-ce que le fuck? "You've got to be kidding," Devlin said incredulously as she got her first look at her "office space."

A tiny desk had been shoved into a storage room. Bankers' boxes were stacked on the desk and all over the floor.

"I'm so sorry." Max looked horrified.

Devlin took a deep breath and slid her laptop bag off her shoulder. She reached inside the room and placed it on top of one of the boxes.

"Don't be. I know exactly how this happened." She smiled at Max and Adrian, and with a shrug, she turned and climbed over the boxes that were blocking the entrance.

She had *many* questions as to why Daniel was being such a jerk, and she knew there were two sides to every story, but in his case, he was definitely the asshole in both of them.

CHAPTER FOURTEEN

When life gives you lemons, squirt them in your enemy's eye.
Devlin was fuming, this was *not* what she expected when
she'd asked to see company records. Daniel had clearly
put a lot of thought into today's campaign of torture.
How had she ever been so delusional as to think there
was a less offensive side to him? Daniel had buried her in
boxes of paperwork, and to top it off, the contents were
all jumbled. Devlin had spent the last two hours trying in
vain to match statements and invoices, vendor
agreements and payment terms, and various banking and
legal documents. Thank Lilith Adrian had stopped by
with a massive cup of coffee. They had turned out to be
Devlin's secret savior!

It had been eerily quiet working in the broom
closet, but that was what you got when you were stashed
away under the stairs. Devlin had actually started to get
into a rhythm as she shifted from box to box when her
concentration was broken by the sound of a squeaking
wheel. She poked her head out of her hidey-hole and
saw someone she'd never met before, wheeling a dolly

stacked with more boxes of files toward her. Devlin felt her irritation morph into a low-grade, simmering rage. She gave the unfortunate delivery person a tense smile as they slid the boxes off the dolly. Her aura must have been pretty dark. She'd never seen someone back away from her that quickly in her life. Drawing on *very* deep reserves of self-control, Devlin lifted the lid off of the top box in the new stack...

Mother F... She ground her teeth to keep the shriek of anger in. The overhead lights in her cramped office flickered madly for a moment as she jammed the top back on the box and took a seat on the tiny stool she'd been given. Devlin rested her elbows on her knees and dropped her head into her hands. *Daniel has his whole life to be an asshole. Why couldn't he have taken today off!?!*

Devlin raised her head at the sound of a new email notification. She reached out and slid her laptop across the tiny desk to read it. The message was from Daniel. He apologized for not meeting her when she arrived (*yeah right*) and was looking forward to their meeting at eleven (*about as much as a root canal*). He wanted to put in a lunch order so it would arrive shortly after their meeting concluded (*food was good*), so could she please let him know what she'd like (*ok, that was actually thoughtful...weird*). Hoping for the best, Devlin fired back a simple reply.

Thank you for ordering lunch. I'm not too picky when it

comes to food, so please go ahead with anything you know is good at whichever restaurant you order from. The only thing I don't like is fish. Thank you!

As she hit Send, Devlin caught the time on the corner of her laptop screen. Sifting through mountains of bullshit had definitely killed most of the morning. It was already almost eleven o'clock, and she had to hustle upstairs for their meeting. Why Daniel had chosen to email her about their lunch order instead of just asking her during their meeting was a mystery, but, hey, if it wasn't another box of files—or hidden coffee—she wasn't about to question it. Devlin shut her laptop, adjusted her hair and outfit, put on her most calm, professional expression, and strode out into the lobby and up the stairs to the second floor.

Thankfully Adrian had pointed out Daniel's temporary office on their Black Ops mission that morning, so Devlin knew exactly where she was headed. His door was closed when she arrived, and she could hear the muted sounds of a conversation. Devlin took a seat in a chair just outside the door to wait...and wait...and wait...

An hour. Devlin was back to simmering rage. She had emailed him, texted him, and knocked on the door. Daniel hadn't so much as acknowledged her presence the entire time she'd waited. This day felt like one of her dad's torture scenarios, and to make things worse, the screen on her phone had been glitching on and off. She was about to get up and bang on his door again when it flew open, and there he was...with his coat on.

"Oh, sorry! I totally forgot about our meeting!" Daniel exclaimed, leaning hard into a melodramatic performance of apology.

"Where are you..." Devlin tried to interject, to no avail.

"I have to step out. Put something in the books for another day and enjoy your lunch!" Daniel shouted as he barreled past her and down the stairs.

Devlin stood rooted to the spot in shock. *What the actual fuck just happened?* There was nothing left for her to do other than return to her storage closet. Devlin walked back down the stairs on auto-pilot.

"Ms. Laflamme?"

Devlin snapped out of her stupor at the sound of Max's voice. "Max, yes, what's up?"

"Mr. Webster wanted to make sure you got your lunch." Max held out a plastic bag that clearly held containers of food.

"Thank you, Max." Devlin reached out and took the bag. Eating her feelings seemed like a good plan.

Devlin collapsed onto her shitty, tiny stool and dropped the bag onto her desk. She attacked the knot tying the plastic handles together like a ravenous beast. When the bag opened, Devlin felt like crying. The smell of fish wafted from the takeout container, filling her tiny faux office and making her stomach turn. Devlin was done. She had no more fucks to give, and her reserves of cheek turning had run empty. She opened her laptop and fired off an email to Daniel.

Daniel, I have spent years dealing with difficult people in boardrooms and being underestimated as a legal professional. The treatment I have received at your hands makes every other experience pale in comparison. I have never felt so disrespected, targeted, and demeaned in a business or personal setting in my life. I will endeavor to conclude business between our companies posthaste in order to minimize and, if possible, eliminate any future interactions. I hope you're proud of yourself. Sincerely, Devlin Laflamme

Devlin slid her laptop back into its bag, put on her coat, and walked out. Dealing with Daniel was like trying to play chess with a pigeon. He just flew around, shitting all over the board and acting like he'd won.

CHAPTER FIFTEEN

The next morning, Devlin had just finished getting dressed and was about to order an Uber to the Harvest Time office when the front desk called. Apparently, Daniel was waiting for her in the lobby. *Curiouser and curiouser.* Devlin shrugged, grabbed her laptop bag, and decided to roll with it...but hung onto a healthy dose of skepticism and anger. What he'd put her through yesterday was the outside of enough, and Devlin was done playing nice. Daniel was about to learn what happened when you poked the beast. She had definitely woken up this morning feeling a lot more like the uber professional, legal powerhouse she was, and Daniel Webster was *not* going to bring her down.

Devlin marched into the lobby with her head held high. Daniel was leaning on the front desk having a chat with the day manager. His head swiveled to face her as the clicking of her heels on the tile floor announced her arrival. She shot him a withering look then shifted her gaze to the manager, pasting on the thousand-watt smile she typically saved for making a good impression schmoozing at cocktail parties she didn't want to be at but had to attend. *Too much?* she thought as the hotel manager looked at her like she was an escaped mental patient. Devlin dialed it down to a five as she got closer.

"Good morning, Daniel." Devlin shot him a very pointed, *what the fuck are you doing here?* look.

His face was frustratingly unreadable. "I figured I'd save you from taking another Uber."

She narrowed her eyes at him, trying to glean the tiniest hint of what Daniel was up to.

"Ready to head out?" He motioned toward his car, parked right outside the double glass doors of the hotel.

Not having much of a choice, Devlin nodded and followed him out. Daniel jogged a few steps to get to the passenger door first, opening it for her to get in.

"Thank you." She heard the words come out sounding more like a question.

Daniel slid into the driver's seat, buckled up, put the key in the ignition...then turned toward Devlin at the exact moment she decided to pipe up.

"About yesterday..." Devlin said, with steel in her voice.

"There's something I'd like to show you," Daniel said in tandem.

"Oh...okay..." Devlin had geared herself up for a fight, not mystery show-and-tell, and didn't know quite what to say.

Instead of driving to the office, Daniel took them into the downtown core, parallel parking in front of a large brick building. Devlin was pissed. She just wanted to get down to business, but her sick sense of curiosity won out. *If it's animal shit again, I'll kill him with my bare hands.*

"Here we are," he said as he unclicked his seatbelt and stepped out of the car.

Devlin got out of the car warily and finally got a look at where they had stopped. The Webster Community Center. She pushed the car door closed and walked closer to the building to read a plaque on the wall near the door. The community center was founded in 1976 by George Webster.

Devlin tensed as she felt Daniel's presence at her side. "He loved this place. He was always trying to get us to spend more time here." He reached out and touched the plaque with reverence.

Despite her irritation at him, Devlin's heart clenched at the sadness in Daniel's voice. She had experienced her mother's passing with the understanding of a child and could only imagine the pain she would feel if her dad were to suddenly disappear from her life now. Lucky for her, the Devil wasn't going anywhere.

Daniel's head was hung in shame as he turned to face her. "I don't have the words to make up for how

I've treated you." He tilted his head toward the plaque. "My father would have been ashamed, and so am I." He shuffled his feet, clearly uncomfortable. "I know I've been a massive dick right from our first email exchange."

Wary, Devlin raised an eyebrow and nodded. "No shit."

"I'm sorry." He didn't try to explain it away or weasel out of it. No excuses, just a simple, unadorned apology.

Devlin wasn't quite sure what to say. The apology didn't fix everything, but it felt like a Band-Aid had been put over the bullet hole, which was better than nothing.

"Can you tell me a bit about the center?" she asked Daniel, genuinely curious to learn more about George and shifting the focus off their interpersonal issues.

Daniel looked at her with gratitude. "The community center offers a series of youth programs, there's a small soup kitchen, and a few beds for emergency housing. Those are mainly filled in the winter because of the cold. Dad never wanted to see anyone hurting when he had the means to help." He reached forward and opened the door. "I'd like to show you around a bit if you're up for it."

Devlin nodded and stepped past him into the building. She actually *was* interested in George Webster's

Community Center. This field trip was infinitely better than spending an entire day in the office sparring with a fractious Daniel.

He perked up instantly as they entered the building. The moment the administrator noticed him, she squealed in delight and ran around the reception desk to grab Daniel in a bear hug.

"Ouff." Daniel had the wind knocked out of him at the sudden love-attack from the tiny powerhouse who had latched on like a barnacle. "Sheila, it's so good to see you!" he squeaked as she squeezed the life out of him.

Sheila released him and took a small step back to look him in the eye. She wagged her finger at him as she scolded. "Daniel Webster, where have you been?"

Daniel stuttered, adjusted his glasses, and ran his fingers through his hair. He shuffled his feet like naughty schoolboy. "I know. I'm sorry. I should have come back sooner."

Devlin chuckled despite herself. Daniel glanced over and gave her an embarrassed, almost shy smile and shrugged.

"Who do we have here?" Sheila noticed Devlin standing off to the side. "Daniel, why have you been hiding this gorgeous woman from us!" She barreled forward to envelop Devlin in her own crushing hug.

Devlin looked over Sheila's head at Daniel,

hoping he could read her silent plea for help.

"Um, yeah, Sheila, Devlin's the lawyer for the firm that's buying my father's business." He stepped forward about to help peel Sheila off her.

Sheila beat him to the punch, stepping away from Devlin like she was a rattlesnake. "*You're* the lawyer."

Here we go again. "Sorry to disappoint." Devlin held up her hands in surrender. "I come in peace."

Sheila's eyes narrowed as she looked at Daniel, then Devlin, then back to Daniel. "Hmmm, we'll see," she said with a raised eyebrow.

Okay... Devlin shot Daniel a confused look. He just shrugged and started moving away from the front desk toward an open door. He motioned for Devlin to join him.

"I promise to have a proper visit very soon, Sheila!"

"Well, off you go then," Sheila muttered as she shooed them away and headed back to the front desk.

"That was interesting," Devlin said as they walked into a large space that was partitioned for different activities.

"Don't mind Sheila." Daniel chuckled. "She's like an aunt. I spent so much time here *she* was the one who made sure I finished my homework and ate all my veggies half the time."

Devlin tapped her chin in mock thought. "So, if I

need to get dirt on you, she would be the one to talk to?"

"Damn it! I should have kept my mouth shut!" he said with feigned horror and a dramatic flourish.

Devlin shook her head in disbelief at the joking version of Daniel. "I think you missed your calling in theater!"

He gave her a cheeky wink. "You're not the first to tell me that." He waved his arm, encompassing the entirety of the enormous room. "Shall we?"

Devlin walked at Daniel's side as he introduced her to the volunteers leading groups and classes for local youth. There was an art class, a computer class, a writing seminar, what looked like a small library, and a dance class. She was so impressed at what George Webster had done here. Everyone was enjoying their time, and every group leader had some memory or story to share about their late patron.

Every so often Devlin caught Daniel looking at her, his eyes searching her face intently. Shockingly, particularly after her treatment the day before, she was finding herself at ease with Daniel Webster. If you'd asked her forty-eight hours ago, she would have told you there were greater odds of being hit by lightning.

When they reached the other end of the space, Daniel pushed open a door to a staircase leading up to a second story.

"I spent a lot of time helping out up here when I

was a teenager." Daniel almost bounced up the stairs with Devlin nipping at his heels. At the landing, Daniel pulled open a heavy wooden door that opened into a full diner-style kitchen.

"Danny!" a large, older gentleman in a chef's jacket exclaimed as he moved toward them with a slow, halting gait.

"Butch." Daniel smiled at him fondly. "How are you doing?" he asked as they leaned in to clap each other on the back.

Butch chuckled and shook his head. "Time stands still for no man. These hips and knees aren't what they used to be. Getting up and down those stairs a couple of times a day is turning into a real chore. I'm not sure how much longer I'll be able to keep working the kitchen here."

"Oh, Butch…" Daniel sighed.

"The place hasn't been the same since your father passed anyhow. Maybe it's time for change around here…some fresh faces." Butch shrugged. "So, are you going to introduce the lovely lady you have with you, or is she in the witness protection program?" He shot Devlin an irreverent wink.

"No, sorry!" Daniel motioned toward Devlin. "Butch, this is Devlin, Devlin, Butch. Butch has been the cook here at our soup kitchen since I can remember."

"It's lovely to meet you." Butch reached out to

shake her hand. "Any friend of Daniel's is a friend of mine."

"Thanks!" Devlin smiled. Butch radiated positive energy. "So, you've known Daniel a long time?"

"I certainly have." Butch motioned for them both to come farther into the room. "Danny boy, why don't you do me a favor and take care of the dishes in that sink." He winked at Devlin. "You can't just come swanning through here without helping out a bit."

Devlin laughed as Daniel rolled his eyes. "Lead me to the battlefield," he said as Butch motioned toward the sink with a flourish. Daniel grabbed a pair of rubber gloves and eyed the *very* large stack of dirty plates and bowls that were overflowing onto the counter tops. "That's a lot of dishes."

Butch shrugged. "Our bus boy couldn't make it in today. He had a hockey tournament out of town."

Daniel got a devilish look in his eye as he snapped on the rubber gloves. "I'm sure Devlin wouldn't want to be deprived of this magical experience, would you, Devlin?" He raised an eyebrow as he looked at her in mock challenge.

"I wouldn't miss it for the world," she retorted as she moved past Daniel to grab the second set of gloves from beside the sink. Her thigh brushed his gently, and Devlin heard him suck in a breath. Her stomach fluttered. *Down, girl! He's still in the dog house!*

With her hands gloved and ready to go, Devlin looked up at Daniel, who raised his hands like a surgeon about to operate.

"Soap, STAT!"

Devlin laughed as she handed him the bottle of dish soap. "Yes, sir!" She couldn't quite believe that they were having a laugh together, when yesterday he had acted like she'd left a grumpy on his favorite rug!

They got to work on the dishes. Daniel was on one side of the double sink scrubbing as Devlin got ready to rinse on the other side. There was just one little problem. While Devlin had done her own cleaning after moving out of her dad's house, she had always had a dishwasher. The damned sink faucet was making her crazy. Figuring out how to pull the spout down was harder than solving a Rubik's Cube, and now she was fiddling around trying to get water out. She pulled the faucet farther out and twisted the hose to the side so she could get a better look at the buttons. *Maybe this one…* She pushed the only button she hadn't tried yet, and water came shooting out. Right. At. Daniel's. Face.

"What the fuck!" Daniel shouted, letting the plate he was holding slide back into the soapy water as he raised his hands to block the water from hitting him right in the kisser.

"Karma," Devlin muttered under her breath as she slowly raised her eyes to look at Daniel's face.

Okay, that is not what I was expecting. Daniel's shoulders were shaking as he peeled off his rubber gloves and tossed them onto the counter. He raised a hand to wipe the water from his eyes and blinked them open. As soon as he saw the horrified expression on Devlin's face, he completely cracked up. Before she could react, Daniel shook his head like a dog, leaning closer to her for maximum spray coverage. Devlin squealed and half hid behind some large crates of produce stacked a few feet back from the sink. She peeked at Daniel from around the side of the tallest crate. Daniel held his hands up in mock surrender, and Devlin slid out from behind her makeshift shield.

"I'm so sorry." She chuckled as she swiped a dishtowel off the counter and handed it to Daniel, who immediately wiped his face and rubbed his hair.

"Don't worry about it." He smiled at her with laughter still in his eyes. "Unless that's your not-so-subtle way of telling me I stink and need a shower?"

Devlin heard the words coming out of her mouth before she had a second to think them through. "No, you smell really good." *Dumbass!* She felt her face flush.

Daniel cleared his throat awkwardly. "Um, uh… thanks?"

It was at that exact moment that Devlin's stomach decided to let out the most ferocious growl she'd ever heard. Hellhounds would have run at that noise!

She had never been so happy to have a bodily function interrupt an awkward moment in her life.

"Come on, let's get you something to eat." Daniel chuckled as he tossed the dishtowel onto the sink. "I'll come back later to finish these dishes off. Just let me leave a note for Butch."

CHAPTER SIXTEEN

"There's a little place just a few doors down that I've always loved," Daniel said as he ushered Devlin out of the community center with a gentle hand on the small of her back.

"As long as they have something more substantial than salad, I'll be happy," Devlin said as her stomach let out another impressive growl. She peeked at her watch and could hardly believe it was already noon!

Daniel laughed. "I think I've got you covered."

As they walked the short distance down the street side-by-side, Devlin had a strange desire to hold Daniel's hand. Something felt so *right* about walking next to him. *Keep your hands and arms inside the ride at all times.* She stuffed her hands into her coat pockets just to be safe.

"Here we are." Daniel motioned to the doorway of a little Italian restaurant.

"Sweet, sweet carbs," Devlin muttered.

Daniel laughed.

"Did I say that out loud?" she asked, embarrassed.

Daniel smiled. "I like a girl that's not afraid of some pasta."

"Then I'll be your favorite person," Devlin promised with mock sincerity.

They were smiling as they walked into the cozy restaurant. The dinging of the little bell above the door attracted the attention of a young woman delivering plates to a nearby table. The second she clapped eyes on Daniel, a giant smile took over her face.

"Danny?" She hurried toward them.

"Little Stephanie?" he asked in confusion and surprise.

"Yes!" She nodded with a huge smile. "You remember me!"

Daniel shook his head in shock. "You're all grown up! Last time I saw you, you were…"

"Twelve," Stephanie cut in. "I'm seventeen now!" She gave him a gentle punch to the arm in jest.

Daniel shook his head, and a touch of sadness slipped into his smile. "It really has been that long, hasn't it? Are you graduating from high school this year?"

"Yup!" She smiled brightly. "I already did some early applications to universities. Hopefully I'll hear back soon!"

"That's amazing!" Daniel turned to Devlin. "Stephanie's mother is one of the administrators at Harvest Time. I used to watch her when her mom needed a hand."

"Ugh," Stephanie groaned. "You make it sound like I was a little kid you were babysitting." She rolled her eyes and turned to Devlin. "I didn't need a babysitter or anything. He was more like a tutor, you know."

Devlin nodded seriously. "Of course, I get it." She almost lost her composure as Daniel choked on a laugh.

"So, is she your girlfriend?" Stephanie asked directly.

Daniel stuttered, and Devlin felt a flutter of... something. She decided to jump in and save him. "No, I'm not his girlfriend. My name is Devlin." She extended her hand to shake Stephanie's. "We're working together."

"Okay," Stephanie said. The answer was clearly enough to satisfy her curiosity on the topic. She turned to the front desk, grabbed a couple of menus off the counter, and motioned for them to walk with her. "This way."

Daniel looked at Devlin and shrugged as they followed her.

Devlin took off her coat and hung it over the back of the chair as she sat at the cozy table. Out of the corner of her eye, she watched as Daniel removed his coat, slung it over his chair, and sat down across from her. This was going to be a series of awkward moments separated by food. She took a deep breath and prayed that they could order fast. Devlin picked up the menu in front of her and busied herself reviewing her pasta options. The menu made a great shield, but she was unable to stop herself from sneaking looks at Daniel, like a creepy Jack-in-the Box clown. Oddly, he seemed to be pulling the exact same routine.

The awkwardness was making Devlin twitchy. She started fidgeting with her earrings, her watch, her hair, basically anything not nailed down. She had reached the end of her tether. *Screw it!* She looked up, determined to put an end to the foolishness, and almost burst out laughing. Daniel was busy mucking about with his hair and repeatedly adjusting his glasses with one hand while holding up his menu with the other. He caught her looking at him and froze. With a sigh, he dropped his menu and placed both hands on it, palms down. Devlin lowered her menu in response, two dueling parties laying down their arms.

"I just want…"

"So, here's the deal…"

They spoke in tandem, breaking the icky, uncomfortable silence.

"You go," Daniel said, motioning for Devlin to speak.

"No, please, you go," Devlin replied, not quite sure what had been about to pop out of her mouth anyhow.

Daniel nodded, and with a wry smile, he picked up his white linen napkin and waved it in surrender.

Devlin chuckled and rolled her eyes. "I second that motion."

Stephanie chose that moment to arrive at their table with a pen and note pad. "Have you had a chance to look at the menu?" she asked Devlin. "I already know what *you* want," she said, shooting Daniel a cheeky look.

"You sure do!" He smiled, handing his menu back to Stephanie. "I'll take the same thing I ordered every time we came here for lunch back in the day!"

"What is it?" Devlin asked. "I might as well get the inside scoop. It must be good!"

"You have no idea!" Daniel gushed. "Grilled chicken caprese. It's to die for!"

Daniel looked like he was about to start drooling, so Devlin figured she couldn't go wrong. "Make that two," she said, handing her menu back to Stephanie.

"Drinks?" Stephanie asked with an eyebrow raise.

Oh, what the hell, it's five o'clock somewhere. Devlin threw caution to the wind. "I'll take a glass of your house red."

"Designated driver here. Just water for me, Steph," Daniel said with a smile.

Stephanie gave Daniel a little salute then whirled around, her ponytail swishing behind her as she sauntered back to the kitchen with their order.

Daniel shook his head and gave Devlin a crooked smile. "She was the cutest kid. She was smart as a whip and funny as hell. It doesn't look like much has changed."

"She certainly seems to have fond memories of you," Devlin said softly.

"About today…" Daniel's expression turned to a mixture of sadness and determination. "I know it probably won't make any difference in the long run, but I did want to show you what Harvest Time meant to the community, what my father meant to the community…to me."

"I get wanting to save your family's legacy, and I can see why." She took a deep breath as she delved into the bad part. "There just isn't anything you can do to stop the sale. Your siblings are in favor…" She trailed off, waiting for the Douchey Daniel to reappear.

"I know." Daniel gave her a sad smile. "I can't keep dragging out the contract negotiations. You're too smart not to have figured out what I was trying to do."

"The revenue clause?" she asked with an eyebrow raise.

"Bingo," Daniel said with a snap and a Fonzie finger-point. "Is there any way you can give me some time to try to meet that threshold? I'd probably be more likely to get hit by lightning, but…"

Devlin's heart twisted a bit looking at the faint

spark of hope in his eyes, but her hands were tied. "They've been chomping at the bit to move the closing of this sale along." She shook her head sadly.

"Seventy-two hours, that's all I'm asking for. Can you buy me three days to try and change their minds? Maybe I can find a way to buy them out or find another investor…" Daniel pleaded.

Just yesterday, Devlin would have reveled in hearing Daniel beg for her help. Now, she wanted to give him what he asked for, if for no other reason than to allow him closure. "Seventy-two hours," she said firmly. "That's all I can reasonably give you without running afoul of my contractual responsibilities."

"I'll take whatever you'll give me." Daniel gave her a grateful smile.

Her wine arrived at the table, and boy did she need it. Devlin was having difficulty reconciling today's feelings of empathy with yesterday's feelings of hostility. Hells bells, this shit was whiplash inducing.

"So…" Devlin swirled the wine in her glass. "What was it like growing up around here?" She was genuinely curious to hear more about *Danny* Webster.

Daniel launched into tales of his youth as their lunch arrived. He talked about working on local farms that supplied the family business during the summers and volunteering at the Community Center during the fall and winter. He and his siblings had been close when they were young, spending time hiking the trails around Duchesnay Falls together and playing hockey at the outdoor arenas. The family cabin by the lake was their chosen hangout with friends during the summer. It sounded like an ideal youth. Daniel finished his story by talking about his acceptance to university and heading off to Toronto to study.

"Now that you know all about me, what about you?" he asked with true interest. "How did Devlin Laflamme wind up working at Obsidian Enterprises? Is your father the Devil incarnate at the office or a big softie?" He smiled at her, cocking his head to the side as he waited to hear her story.

Devlin almost spit out her wine. *If you only knew...* She chuckled to herself as she launched into a mortal-friendly, curated version of life with dear old dad. She told Daniel how close they became after her mother's death and how hard it was on him to step away when she went off to university. She talked about the student loan she'd taken out instead of relying on daddy's money and the thankless job she'd worked in a call center to pay for her room and board. Devlin could tell he was surprised, and if she wasn't mistaken, she saw a hint of admiration as well. *Put that in your pipe and smoke it!* Devlin thought with satisfaction as she remembered his "silver spoon" comment in her office.

To Devlin's surprise, they were vibing really well,

the conversation flowed easily, and they connected through a lot of shared experiences in law school. If only Daniel would stop distracting her, putting his glasses on, taking them off, fiddling with them a bit, then putting them back on... *Clark Kent, Superman, Clark Kent, Superman... Business lunch, not a date, business lunch, not a date.* Devlin repeated that mantra over and over in an effort to keep her thoughts at a PG rating.

As their meal drew to a close, she offered to pay, but Daniel wasn't hearing it.

"Don't be silly." He shook his head. "I invited you, so I get first dibs on the check." He smiled and tossed his credit card onto the tray.

Devlin was able to get on board with that logic, and relented, but she noticed he hadn't taken out a corporate card. Daniel was using his personal credit card. *Don't be reading into things. He probably doesn't have a corporate card. It's just a business lunch. Snap out of it!*

Devlin grabbed her coat off the back of her chair. Before she had time to twist her arms around to shrug it on, Daniel was there, taking the coat out of her hands and holding it up for her to slip into gracefully. *Classy,* she noted. As they headed out to his car, Daniel took her elbow gently as they picked their way down the treacherous, freshly salted sidewalk. *Note to self—must buy flat boots!*

As they got to his car, Daniel opened the

passenger door and held it for her as she slid in. A moment later he was sitting beside her in the driver's seat. They shivered in the car as it warmed up before they could drive away.

"I'm sorry." Daniel scrunched his face in embarrassment. "I should have used the remote starter before we left the restaurant. What an idiot!"

"It's all good," Devlin reassured him while marveling that even her internal organs were shivering!

Daniel must have assessed the threat-level of arctic air blasting through the radiator to be sufficiently reduced. He reached forward and twisted the knob on the heater to full blast. He grabbed the gear shifter and put the car in Drive then changed his mind and returned the car to Park.

"Devlin?" He turned to her with a nervous, questioning look. "I have a few things I need to take care of during the day tomorrow…bank visits, talking to a few potential investors…but would you maybe be up for doing something tomorrow evening?"

Devlin's stomach fluttered. She hadn't felt like this in who knows how long, and she liked it. "Um, yeah, sure, sounds good." She turned to him, suddenly feeling shy, but that shyness turned to something entirely different when she caught Daniel's eye.

If looks could start forest fires, this one would be a raging inferno. Devlin felt her body melt. She swayed a fraction closer to him as though she was being magnetically pulled. He looked like he was imagining all the things he wanted to do to her in the dark.

The radio suddenly clicked on, flipping madly through the stations like it was possessed.

"What the fuck?" Daniel snapped out of the heated trance and twisted the knobs on the radio, smacking the console to see if he could beat it into submission.

Easy, girl. Devlin tried to calm the heady buzz she felt running through her body. Her efforts were in vain. The only thing she wanted to do was...well...Daniel. Devlin felt like she was going to combust. She rested her forehead against the freezing window and focused on her breath. Slowly but surely the feeling receded until it was just a gnawing ache inside of her.

"There we go!" Daniel exclaimed with satisfaction as the radio finally shut off. "I have no idea what's going on with this stupid thing. Gotta get it looked at."

Devlin plastered on her calmest smile. "Good plan," she said, hoping he couldn't see how hot and bothered he'd made her. *#cringe* The afternoon at the office was going to be super fun.

CHAPTER SEVENTEEN

The *ding ding* of incoming text messages woke Devlin the next morning. She rolled over and stretched herself out like a cat. With a resigned sigh, she finally opened her eyes and squinted at the bedside clock. Ten o'clock! *Holy shit!* She hadn't slept in this late on a weekday in years! *How the fuck did this happen?* Another glance at the alarm answered *that* question. She'd set the alarm for pm, instead of am. That was a first! Devlin popped upright, swung her legs over the side of the bed and stood there in a panic trying to figure out what she was late for. Her pounding heart started to slow as the realization dawned on her that, for once in her life, she had nowhere to be. She had no meetings planned at Harvest Time and no video conferences in her calendar. The fight-or-flight drained out of her system, and she plopped back down onto the edge of her bed. *Now what?*

As she glanced around her room, hoping for some sort of inspiration on how to spend her day, Devlin's eyes landed on her suitcase. She still needed a warmer coat and a pair of flat boots if she planned on spending a few more days in North Bay. Her stomach growled angrily. *You can never go wrong with a muffin and a cappuccino.* A trip to her new favorite café and a chat with Diane sounded like a great start.

Devlin took her time getting dressed. She had never been a morning person, so it was really nice to not have to put on her "competent lawyer" persona. Having a lazy morning where there were zero expectations of her time was novel, and something she could get used to!

As she finished putting her hair up into a ponytail, Devlin realized she hadn't bothered to check the texts that had so rudely woken her. She grabbed and unlocked her phone. Normally that little *ding* had her jumping like Pavlov's dog. Unless she was in a meeting or in court, she was on it in a flash. This really *was* shaping up to be a different sort of morning!

One message was from Kitty. It seemed Daniel's siblings were stressing her out trying to get information on the delay in closing the sale. Devlin texted her a string of legal word-salad that sounded legit enough to put off any more immediate questions. Kitty would get the picture and use her text word-for-word to respond to their inquiry. Daniel's siblings weren't the type of folks who would cop to not understanding legal jargon; they were just that narcissistic!

The second message was from Daniel. He was checking in to see if they were still on for their get-together that evening. Her heart skipped, and she felt low-grade butterflies in her stomach as she replied. She tried to sound blasé as she answered in the affirmative, reading her response a half-dozen times before hitting Send just to be sure.

Devlin started to feel the early twinges of a caffeine headache coming on. That trip to Diane's café was now a medical necessity. She grabbed her jacket and headed out. The bitter cold wind that whipped at her as she stepped outside always managed to take her breath away. She shook her head at her own stupidity. How had it not occurred to her to bring a proper coat? She would definitely be in line for a Darwin Award after this trip.

She shoved her hands under her armpits and charged down the street. She kept her head down and her eyes peeled for those hellish little chunks of salt that spelled doom if they were stepped on in *just* the wrong way. She'd started feeling like she had it down to a fine art. *The newest Winter Olympic sport, The Salt Run!* Devlin figured she'd be able to win that event by a landslide after all the training she'd gotten this week!

If this was a sport, then the door to the café was the finish line, and Devlin had never been happier to step across a threshold! Diane looked up and greeted her with a smile, pointing toward the table they'd sat at before. There was a lineup at the counter. Diane passed takeaway cups and bags to patrons, moving quickly to make sure nobody waited too long. Devlin nodded as Diane flashed a hand toward her, showing five fingers. It looked like people were picking up their mid-morning caffeine fixes on their breaks. A few patrons turned to look at Devlin. There weren't any dirty looks this time, just naked curiosity.

Diane passed her last customer a bag and a cup, waving at him as he adjusted his scarf and headed out the door.

She turned to Devlin. "Pick your poison." She smiled.

"A cappuccino would be great," Devlin said as she got up and walked to the counter. She scanned the display case to see what types of muffins were left. "Hmmm...I'd also love a red velvet muffin." Her stomach growled in agreement.

"Coming right up!" Diane said as she got to work behind the counter, the sounds of frothing and steaming filled the air.

Moments later, a cup of liquid gold slid across the counter, followed by a saucer with the most perfectly formed muffin Devlin had ever seen. The cream cheese icing was calling to her like a siren.

Diane came around the counter and waved for Devlin to follow her back to the table. "You're a hot topic today," she said as they sat down.

Devlin frowned. "What do you mean?" She took a sip of her drink.

"Did you forget you were hanging out with a local celebrity yesterday?" Diane chuckled. "All eyes were on you two, and nobody has seen Daniel happy since he's been home. Not to mention, he's taking you to some of his favorite places."

"The community center?" Devlin asked.

"Everywhere you've been. He spent a lot of time with his father at Joe's farm, the community center, the restaurant you ate at is his favorite..." Diane trailed off as she raised her own mug to her lips, keeping an eye on Devlin's reaction over the rim of her cup.

"Hunh..." Devlin wasn't quite sure how to feel. The farm torture was...what? "Daniel has been pretty irked at me because of the business, but surely, he hasn't been miserable with everyone..."

"I'll get to that in a minute, but first thing's first. Spill, are you two..." Diane wiggled her eyebrows suggestively. "Have you been going through more than *legal* briefs?"

Devlin choked on her cappuccino, coughing and spluttering before she was able to get words out. "No, no! Nothing like that!" she insisted. "Is that what everyone thinks?" she asked with a touch of horror in her voice. Devlin blushed furiously as her brain started to spin. *How unprofessional!* She had *never* done anything to raise an eyebrow in her career, and here she was with a whole *town* thinking there was something going on between her and Daniel. To be fair, he wasn't *exactly* a client, since he hadn't been involved in the sale directly, but still...

"How bad is it?" Devlin whispered in distress.

"Don't worry!" Diane reached out to pat Devlin's hand reassuringly. "Nobody's looking negatively on it, but rumor around town is that you two looked pretty happy...and cozy together at lunch yesterday."

"It was just a business lunch!" Devlin insisted.

"Un hunh," Diane said with a wink and a nod, taking another leisurely sip of her drink.

Devlin sighed in resignation. "It was a good lunch. We had a good day actually. He was different from how he's been. I just can't seem to figure him out, which is really frustrating. I've always read people pretty easily. It comes in handy in my line of work." She sipped her cappuccino, her thoughts fixed on Daniel and the personality transplant he'd undergone. "He was basically Oscar the Grouch for weeks, and then yesterday, he turned into a totally different person, someone I actually enjoyed spending time with. Nothing has materially changed about our situation. The sale of the company is still happening, I'm still working for the company that's buying—"

"I wish I could tell you all about Daniel, but it's

his story, and it isn't my place to share. I will say that he's a good man. He always has been. It's been a rough few years for him, but I can promise you that the guy you saw at your *business lunch* is the real Daniel Webster. I just don't want to see him get hurt," Diane said pointedly.

"I get the feeling you're right about that...the good man thing," Devlin replied softly.

They sat in silence for a while, both women lost in thought. Devlin mindlessly ate her muffin, barely tasting the icing. It was Diane that broke the silence.

"So, what are your plans for today? Are you going back to the Harvest Time office?" She picked up the cups and plates, moving them to the counter behind the till.

"No," Devlin said as she stood and slipped on her coat, digging in her purse to grab her wallet. "I'm actually taking the day off. I do have plans to meet up with Daniel later." She felt the blush creep back up her cheeks.

Diane waved Devlin off as she held up a debit card to pay for her breakfast. "It's on the house. Consider it a perk of being friends with the owner."

"Thank you." Devlin smiled. "Friends...I like it! You have no idea how grateful I am to have met you!"

Devlin stopped on her way to the door and turned back. "What are the odds someone at a store around here will actually let me in to buy a coat at this point?" Diane laughed as Devlin continued. "I've been running around freezing my ass off! The two coats I brought are *not* made for North Bay winters, and one of them is at the cleaners because it reeks of cow shit! I'm used to jumping in and out of company cars or going from underground parking to underground parking!" At this point both women were laughing at the absurdity of her situation.

"Well…" Diane was still cackling as she replied. "You'll probably see a change in how you're received today, now that you've had some good PR!"

Devlin threw up her hands and shrugged. "I'll take it for a win."

Time to buy a warmer coat. Her daily impressions of a chattering-teeth toy were getting kinda long in the tooth… Har, har!

CHAPTER EIGHTEEN

Wear something warm and comfortable. That was all Daniel's text had said. She stood there in her underwear, shaking her head. She shot a frustrated look at her phone as it sat charging on the bedside table of her hotel room. *Very helpful, Daniel, a tiny spoiler would have been great!* She puffed out a breath and attacked her suitcase in earnest. There had to be something other than pajamas covered in cartoon sheep that she could wear! Daniel's text had come too late for her to go back to the store for another round of shopping, so she had to make do with what she'd brought. She dug through a pile of tailored pants and fitted dresses, shaking her head. If *this* wasn't a flashing neon sign that she needed to get a life outside of the office, she didn't know what was. *All work and no play makes Devlin a wardrobe-challenged girl!* She was half considering texting Daniel back to poke for more information on their destination when her hand touched a pair of gray dress pants that had a bit more give in the material. They were her "comfy" work pants, the ones she hauled out when she felt gross. It was meant to be a quick trip, but she'd learned early in her career to plan for anything. *Except winter it seems.* So, the "period pants" were a staple when she traveled. She'd never been so happy for her over-the-top packing!

Devlin grabbed the pants and moved on to the closet, sliding open the mirrored door. She began flipping past dress shirt and after dress shirt until she found the one sweater she'd brought with her. It was a soft red cashmere that made the green of her eyes pop, like she was a walking Christmas tree. She smiled as she pulled the sweater on. *Onto hair and makeup!* Devlin shut the closet door and stared at her reflection. Her hair was still in a ponytail from the morning, and there wasn't a stitch of makeup on her face. She never left the house without makeup on and her hair done, but for some reason, as she stared at her bare face and pulled-back hair, she didn't want to change a thing. *Not half bad, kid.*

With a smile of anticipation, she threw on her brand-new flat-soled hiking boots and the red winter jacket she'd spotted in the shop window. *Good choice,* she thought as she took in the whole effect in the closet door. She was too antsy to wait in her room for the concierge to call, so she headed down to the lobby to pace the marble floor in view of the doors. Throughout her lazy day, Devlin had found her thoughts turning to Daniel more often than was healthy. She had finally admitted to herself that she wanted to spend more time with him, which was weird, but what the hell! She had started to think that she was more likely to find Waldo than a man that really turned her crank!

Her heart skipped a beat when Daniel's car pulled up in front of the glass double doors of the hotel. He jumped out and came around to open the passenger door the moment he saw Devlin walking out to meet him. Daniel looked nervous. He smiled at her almost shyly. Their eyes met, and both of them glanced away at light speed. *This feels like a date.* A nervous fluttering took up residence in her stomach. Devlin slid into the passenger seat and got herself situated as Daniel went back around to the driver's side and got in.

Before putting the car in gear, Daniel turned to her with a shy smile. "I want to take you to another place I love around here, an outdoor skating rink not too far from the lake."

Devlin pasted on a happy smile, hoping she'd hit the right level of "yay," but her thoughts went straight to, *oh fuck!* She had always prided herself on being a pretty self-aware person, and she was one hundred percent certain that sports were not her strong suit. Grace and coordination were not her friends. She had only gone skating once in her life, and it hadn't been her finest moment. She gulped nervously. This was going to be a shitshow!

CHAPTER NINETEEN

The skating oval had a backdrop of trees and fairy lights that twinkled in the twilight. There were several couples already on the ice, holding hands and laughing as they skated. *It looks like a date spot...* Daniel had clearly planned this expedition well. When they parked next to the oval, he opened the trunk and pulled out a pair of skates he'd borrowed from the sister of an old friend. They walked to a bench that sat right at the edge of the ice, and Daniel motioned for Devlin to sit.

"I guessed the size," he said as he sank down to kneel at her feet.

Devlin sucked in a breath as he reached out to take her booted foot. "May I?" he asked, lifting his eyes to meet hers. All she could do was nod mutely; her voice had taken an unplanned vacation.

Daniel got to work unlacing her boots and slipping on the borrowed skates, making sure they were snug and comfortable. Devlin sat there, completely flustered in the middle of her own personal Cinderella moment.

"How do they feel?" Daniel asked as his eyes moved back to meet hers.

"They're a perfect fit," she said incredulously.

With a reluctant look, Daniel released her foot and took a seat on the bench beside her. He slipped on his skates and laced them quickly and efficiently. All booted up, Daniel stepped onto the ice smoothly and confidently. He turned to face Devlin and extended his gloved hand to her.

"I'm a terrible skater...two left feet," she warned, looking up at him nervously.

"I'll catch you if you fall."

Something in the way he said it made her believe in him. With a deep breath she took his hand. She stood on shaky legs like a newborn foal, and Daniel wrapped a steady, comforting arm around her. He held her close as she stepped onto the ice. His warmth was reassuring, and the smell of his cologne was intoxicating. She leaned into him a bit more than she needed to.

"How are you feeling?" Daniel asked as they slowly made their way out into the oval.

"Shockingly, I'm actually doing okay, but don't let me go." She peeled her eyes away from the ice in front of her to look up at him.

"I won't." Daniel pulled her closer instinctively.

He breathed deeply, and Devlin suspected he was taking in her scent, which gave her a little thrill. *Welcome to the club, buddy!*

As Devlin's balance got better, Daniel slipped his arm out from around her and turned to skate backward, facing her. He took her hands in his to give her extra stability as she moved slowly, but more steadily, across the ice.

"So, you did a lot of skating growing up?" she asked him, her eyes flicking from the ice to his face and back again.

"Just keep looking at me. It will help your balance." Daniel waited for her eyes to meet his and stay put before responding. "My brothers and I played hockey at one of the other outdoor rinks. I came to this one by myself. I like the trees, and it was always peaceful to skate around and spend some time in my own head."

"Hmmm. I had a place like that too. I mean it wasn't outdoors, or sports related in any way, but I used to go into my dad's library. I've always loved to read, and there is a massive wooden table I used to sit under with a little lamp and a blanket. It was cozy and quiet and all mine." Devlin smiled fondly at the memory.

"So, what about now?" he asked.

She cocked her head. "What do you mean?"

"What do you do when you're not busy working? What do you get up to on the weekends?" He raised an eyebrow.

Devlin's Spidey senses were tingling big time.

This kinda felt like he was fishing to learn more than whether she did yoga on Saturdays. Feeling bold, Devlin decided to respond with a question of her own.

"Daniel, why did you invite me out tonight?"

A blush raced up his neck at record speed. His eyes drifted away briefly before returning to search her face. Devlin didn't let her gaze wander. Well, until he licked his lips, drawing her eyes down to his mouth. Neither of them was paying attention to their surroundings as they moved across the ice perilously close to the edge of the oval. It was Daniel's blade that ran off the ice into the snow first, throwing him off balance. He fell backward, taking Devlin down with him. They landed on the soft snow; Devlin's fall was broken by Daniel's body.

They lay there laughing at their less-than-graceful splat into the snow. Devlin propped herself up with one hand in an effort to take some of her weight off Daniel's chest. She shifted slightly, drawing a sharp breath from Daniel when her lower body slid against his. Devlin froze, staring right into his eyes. They were dilated like saucers and boring into hers with an intensity that made her shiver.

"I told you I'd catch you," he whispered as he reached a hand up to tuck an errant hair behind her ear.

Definitely a date.

Fireworks. They collided in a blistering kiss.

Daniel's hand slid around the back of Devlin's neck, pulling her toward him as he lifted his upper body from the ground to close the distance. The air around them sizzled with electricity as Devlin wrapped an arm around him, crushing his body to hers. He was sitting up as Devlin straddled his waist. Her free hand slid up his bicep to his neck, wrapping around the base of his skull. Her fingers speared into his hair as their lips parted. Their tongues touched, sliding against each other sensuously as the kiss deepened. Devlin pressed herself down into Daniel's lap, rubbing against him. They moaned. This kiss had become the outlet for all the built-up hate, irritation, and tension between them.

Oblivious to the world around them, Daniel grabbed Devlin's ass and pulled her harder against him. She freed one of her hands to roam the front of his coat, tugging buttons and zippers, trying to gain access. All she wanted in that moment was to have her hands on Daniel's bare skin. Flashes and pops of light went off like little fireworks, catching their attention. The fairy lights in the trees exploded and sparked, leaving the area around them blanketed in shadows. Devlin heard surprised shrieks and muffled voices as the other skaters started carefully making their way off the ice in the dark. She had been so wrapped up in the moment she'd forgotten they were smack-dab in the middle of a public park. It seemed they'd lucked out with their little tryst being unobserved. Devlin's breath sawed in and out as she leaned her forehead against Daniel's. They held each other close as they recovered their breath.

"I wonder what happened to the lights. Must be some kind of power surge," Daniel mumbled as he pulled away slightly to cup her face and search her eyes in the moonlight. "You're so beautiful," he said with awe in his voice.

"You're not so bad yourself," Devlin chuckled in embarrassment. "Do you really want this?" Devlin asked, hoping he would reply in the affirmative. All she wanted to do was stay in this little bubble of passion with Daniel.

"Hell yes, from the first moment I saw you in your office!" Daniel's hands twitched on her body, as though it was taking all of his strength to hold them in place. "Just not here." He laughed, glancing around the park.

Devlin chuckled in agreement. "No kidding. I'm not super interested in explaining public indecency charges to the Law Society."

He nodded. "Don't get disbarred...solid plan!"

Devlin crawled off Daniel's lap, and they rose to their feet. She looked around to get her bearings and realized they were pretty close to the bench where they'd started. She poked Daniel's arm to get his attention and pointed it out. Not losing another second, he swept her up into his arms. Devlin squeaked as she was lifted into the air, wrapping her arms around his neck and burying her face in his chest. He marched through the snow in his skates, carrying her like a bride.

Daniel set her down when they got to the bench. They unlaced their skates and jammed their feet into their boots as fast as humanly possible.

"My hotel?" Devlin asked.

"I'm staying at the family cabin near the lake. It's not far from here. We'll have less questions to answer if there aren't front desk agents seeing us heading to your room together..." He trailed off.

"Sold!" Devlin grabbed his arm to yank him off the bench. She was far too horny to be screwing around negotiating logistics!

They hustled to Daniel's car, high-stepping through the snow drifts like prize ponies. *Royal Ascot, here we come!* Daniel dug around in his pocket for keys, popping the trunk while on the move so they could drop their skates in and get on the road. He practically threw open the passenger door for Devlin to jump in. He ran around the front of the car, sliding on the snow-covered ice, catching himself on the hood of the car with a priceless "oh shit" look. She snickered.

"Bite me." Daniel laughed as he finally managed to open his door.

The moment his butt hit the seat, Daniel grabbed her in a quick, passionate kiss, like the two-minute run had been more time away from her lips than he could bear. He tore himself away with a frustrated growl. Devlin sympathized one hundred percent. She was slick, hot, and wanted him more than anyone she could remember. Her hand latched onto his thigh as he fumbled with the car keys, dropping them more than once.

"For fuck's sake!" he mumbled over and over as he scrabbled around on the floor, finally grasping the keys and fitting them into the ignition.

The radio came on and immediately started glitching, changing stations at the speed of light.

"What the hell?" Daniel smacked the console. "Why does that keep happening?"

"Fuck it." Devlin reached forward to twirl the volume knob all the way down, killing the infernal noise.

"Yes, let's," Daniel growled. The look he gave her could have melted the polar ice caps. His jaw clenched as he tried to keep himself under control.

He put the car in Drive and punched the gas. *He's going to burn me up and leave nothing behind.* Devlin smiled in anticipation. *Burn, baby, burn!*

CHAPTER TWENTY

One agonizing stop at a convenience store later, Daniel's car pulled into the driveway of the cabin. They reached for each other immediately. Devlin was on fire. If Daniel wanted to get down in the car like a pair of horny teenagers, she was there for it! The bucket seats were not exactly sex-friendly, and Devlin pined for the bench seating of the ancient beater she'd driven when she was in college. Daniel leaned over her, kissing his way down her neck as he tried to find the button to lower her seat.

"Youch!" he shouted as his knee bashed against the dashboard. He reeled back, trying to balance himself with a hand but misjudged the distance and leaned on the horn. "Fuck!" he muttered as the sound blared in the night.

Devlin was frustrated as hell but couldn't stop herself from cracking up at the absurdity of two thirty-somethings fumbling around in a car like they were sneaking around, hiding from their parents.

"Screw it." Daniel threw open his door and got out, making a move to circle around to Devlin's side, but she'd already beaten him to it.

"That's the plan." Devlin gave him a devilish wink as she slid out of the car and closed the door. She ran to the door of the cabin with Daniel hot on her heels. He caught her and wrapped one arm around her from behind, pulling her body flush against his. Devlin dropped her head to the side as he nuzzled her neck, shivering as goosebumps popped up all over her body. Daniel tried in vain to fit the key into the cabin door with his free hand, but the distraction of Devlin's ass pressed against his cock made him drop the keys onto the gravel.

"Damn it," he bit out as he released Devlin and dug around in the tiny stones until he got hold of his keys.

He finally managed to get the key into the lock and pushed the door open. They stumbled inside, clinging to each other for dear life. Daniel kicked the door closed and went to drop the keys on the hall table, but they clattered to the floor when Devlin drew his head down. Her nails scraped up the back of his neck as she tunneled her fingers into his hair. Their lips met in a bruising kiss. She tore herself away from him to unzip her winter coat and let it drop to the floor at her feet. She bent down to unlace her boots, tugging them off one by one. As she stood, she saw Daniel's coat go flying in the air into the adjoining room, landing half-on, half-off a couch. His boots smacked the closet door as he kicked them off before reaching for her again. He slid a hand up Devlin's back, plastering her against him. She felt his rock-hard cock pressing against her belly. *Someone's happy to see me.* She sighed, her lips parting to allow his tongue in to tangle with hers. Liquid fire pooled between her legs as she rubbed her breasts against Daniel's chest. Her nipples were so hard they could cut glass.

They pulled apart to suck in some much-needed oxygen. "So, a gentleman would ask you if you wanted a drink…" Daniel started as his breath sawed in and out.

"Good thing I'm not looking for you to be a gentleman right now." Devlin stepped back into his body, plastering herself against him like a second skin.

"Thank God for that," Daniel said as Devlin tilted her hips into his and nipped at his lower lip, making him groan.

"Well, maybe not him," Devlin mumbled. "Bedroom?" she whispered as she gave Daniel's earlobe a love bite.

He shivered in pleasure as he pointed absently behind him. She drove Daniel backward. Their bodies were so close they stumbled over each other, bumping against the back of a couch, a side table, and the wall near the bedroom door. A lamp tilted perilously before righting itself, and pictures rattled on the wall. Devlin had never felt this level of desperation before. She needed to feel his skin against hers like she needed her next breath.

As they fumbled their way into the dim bedroom, Devlin started working on Daniel's shirt. She blew out a frustrated breath as the tiny buttons refused to cooperate. She felt him toss something toward the bed. Her body jerked as Daniel's hand slid up under her sweater, touching the skin of her bare back. She heard the top button of his shirt ping as it popped out of its mooring and hit a hard surface somewhere in the room.

One down, waaaay too many to go. Forcing herself to focus, she made short work of the remaining buttons. Daniel slid his hand from under her top and helped her out by slowly unbuttoning his cuffs, his eyes locked on hers. Devlin licked her lips and reached out to push his shirt over his shoulders, watching as it slid down his arms. Daniel's chest was now bare to her greedy eyes in the moonlight filtering through the open window, and she wasn't disappointed. Her hands itched to touch him, and she wasn't about to deny herself. It had been a *very* long time. She hadn't had a partner in a couple of years, not since she had gotten bored of swiping right. Daniel was *exactly* the right person to break her fast with. *If Daniel was a fruit, he'd definitely be a fineapple!*

Devlin marveled at how Daniel managed to look lean and professorly, buttoned up and polished one minute and like a tousled comic book hero the next.

"Damn," she breathed in approval.

"Thanks." Daniel smiled awkwardly for such a hot man. "Do I get a turn?" he asked as his eyes roamed over her, stopping on her breasts. She knew her nipples *must* be giving him a serious show.

Daniel grasped the bottom of her sweater and drew it slowly up her body, revealing it inch by inch. Devlin sucked in a breath as the soft material slipped over her achingly sensitive nipples, exposing them to the cool air.

"No bra," Daniel breathed in approval.

"They're uncomfortable," Devlin whispered as her sweater continued its slow journey upward.

She closed her eyes as the material slid gently over her face and head and lowered her arms to let the sweater slip down onto the floor. She stood, naked from the waist up as Daniel's fevered gaze devoured her. She had never felt so desirable. He laid his palm just below her collarbone and slowly dragged it down, between her breasts then lower until he reached the button of her pants, toying with it but not popping it open. Her skin tingled in the wake of his touch. Daniel's teasing was driving her crazy. Unable to keep her hands off him, Devlin reached out, grasping his forearms and sliding her hands slowly up his arms, feeling the tensing and flexing of his biceps.

Daniel's control snapped. He lifted Devlin into his arms and walked the few feet to the bed, laying her out like a sacrifice. She ran the tips of her fingers down her stomach toward her belly button. Daniel knelt on the edge of the bed, his eyes following the movement of her hand as it trailed down her body. She shivered as he crawled toward her like an animal who had cornered its prey.

"May I?" he growled as he straddled her legs. He leaned forward to kiss and lick her belly button as he waited for her reply.

"Yes," Devlin squeaked, doing her best not to squirm as Daniel's tongue circled her sensitized skin.

He glanced up at her with a look that promised no mercy as he made short work of the button and zipper of her pants. He grasped the waistband and dragged them down her legs slowly and torturously, rising to his knees and lifting her legs one by one to slip them off. Devlin heard her pants hit the floor. He grasped one of her legs and leaned forward, hooking her knee over his shoulder. With a wolfish smile, he leaned forward and dragged his tongue up the inside of her thigh. Devlin squirmed with a combination of anticipation and desperation. She moaned and speared her fingers into his hair, desperate to find some sort of anchor. She felt a flood of warmth between her legs and looked down the length of her body to watch Daniel as he locked in on her expression. He hooked one finger under the elastic of her panties and pulled them to the side. With a growl he slid his tongue into her sensitized channel and dragged it through her core as she moaned in pleasure.

Devlin threw her head back and stared at the ceiling, unseeing, as her back arched. Daniel wedged his shoulders in farther between her legs, allowing him to lay his hand on her stomach, holding her in place. Devlin felt his breath tickling her swollen flesh as she lay there, splayed open for him. She released his hair to clutch at the bedcover, balling it in her fists as she waited for his next move, and she didn't have to wait long. Devlin felt the tip of Daniel's tongue penetrate her opening, sliding into her channel as he teased her tight bud with the fingers of his free hand.

"Fuck, yes," she moaned, fisting the bedspread even harder.

Her breathing began to come in shorter, faster puffs as Devlin got closer and closer to climax. Daniel continued to slip his tongue in and out slowly and torturously, keeping her pinned to the bed.

"Not yet," Daniel breathed against her quivering core. "You taste like sin," he groaned, giving her another swift lick.

"Don't stop," she begged, looking at him with pure desperation. She was so close to bliss that if he stopped, she felt like she would die.

Daniel replied with a devilish look. "As you wish."

She felt him shift slightly then a pressure between her legs as he slid a finger inside her. She sighed as the empty feeling was chased away.

"How does that feel?" Daniel asked as he slowly moved his finger.

"So good." She watched the hypnotic movement of his arm going back and forth as he pushed in and out.

"You're so tight," he bit out as he slipped a second finger in.

Daniel dipped his head back down and flicked his tongue over her tight bud, sucking it into his mouth as he thrust his fingers in and out, faster and faster. He took his hand off of her stomach, grabbing onto her upper thigh and opening her up further. Devlin began to writhe beneath him. She raised herself up on her elbows to get a better view as he worked her body. She pumped her hips in time with his thrusts. He looked up at her, and their eyes locked. That was what pushed Devlin over the edge —Daniel's feral eyes as he feasted on her body.

"Fuck! Daniel!" she shouted as she came, twitching and writhing as he slowed the motion of his hand and mouth.

With a self-satisfied smile, Daniel slid his fingers out of her and rose to his knees. Without breaking eye contact, he lifted his fingers to his mouth and licked. *So hot.* Devlin shuddered.

She reached for Daniel. "I need you inside me."

He was happy to oblige. He unzipped his pants. Devlin raised an eyebrow when he shoved them down over his ass and his cock stood at attention. *Commando! I'd never have guessed!* Without missing a beat, Daniel positioned his body between her legs and leaned over her...waaaay over her. *What the...? Oh yeah.* She heard the rustling of a bag as Daniel grabbed the condoms he'd tossed in earlier. The sound of the cardboard box being shredded open made it pretty clear that he was just as eager as she was. Devlin didn't want to contemplate the mutual blue-balling they would have experienced if that convenience store had been out of raincoats.

Daniel righted himself, a condom in hand. He ripped the condom wrapper open with his teeth, pulling it out and rolling it onto his cock. With its party outfit on, Daniel slipped the head of his cock into her folds, rubbing it in her slickness. As Devlin began to lose herself in the sensation, Daniel took both of her hands in his and raised her arms above her head, pinning her gently, but firmly to the mattress. He slowly pushed the tip of his cock into her then withdrew. It was slow torture for both of them as he repeated the action over and over. His jaw was tight with the strain of remaining in control. Devlin whimpered, her body begging to be filled.

"Now?" Daniel asked through gritted teeth.

Devlin nodded, dying to grab his hips as he thrust

forward but unable to. He buried himself to the hilt and froze, remaining still inside her. Devlin felt her body clenching and rippling around his cock as it pulsed in time with his heartbeat.

"You feel so good," Daniel moaned on a shuddering breath.

"Please…" she begged, desperate for him to move.

"Not yet." Daniel grasped both of her wrists in one hand, freeing the other to pinch and tease one of her nipples.

Devlin cried out; goosebumps broke out across her breasts. "You're a sadist."

Daniel chuckled. "Maybe a bit of a control freak, but hardly a sadist."

He lowered his mouth to her other breast and licked around her nipple as he continued teasing the first. The air was cold on her damp skin. Devlin shivered as she lay helpless to the onslaught of pleasure. He sucked her nipple into his mouth, rolling his tongue around the tip and giving it a tiny nip as he withdrew to take a look at his handywork. Devlin knew she must have looked like a madwoman, but Daniel was clearly happy with what he saw.

"Are your wrists okay?" he asked.

Devlin was so far-gone all she could do was nod. Daniel pulled his hips back, almost withdrawing from her completely.

"Oh fuck, I can't..." he mumbled as he finally lost control.

Daniel's body pistoned back and forth as he abandoned himself to his most basic instincts. Devlin threw her head back as she felt her hips rising to meet his thrusts of their own accord. Her raised arms kept her breasts high, her nipples being teased by occasional brushes of Daniel's chest. He released one of her wrists, taking her hand in his and guiding it down her body between her legs as he continued to thrust into her.

"Touch yourself," he commanded.

Damn you, you cocky prick. She quite happily complied. Her fingers danced over her slick flesh. Her breathing became more and more erratic as waves of pleasure crashed over her. Devlin had never experienced such an intense, rolling tide of sensation with any other partner. It felt like her heart could actually give out. *What a way to go.* This whole experience felt like one unending climax that ebbed and peaked over and over. Her throat was hoarse from her cries.

Daniel growled above her as he pounded his cock into her again and again. He grasped her under one of her knees, shifting her hips upward and deepening his thrusts. The pleasure she felt increased exponentially, lifting her to a peak she'd never experienced before. She felt her channel twitching and gripping his cock as the sensation spread out from her core through her entire body.

"Fuck!" Devlin cried out as the orgasm slammed through her, not once but multiple times as he continued to thrust into her wildly.

"Devlin!" he shouted as his hips moved more erratically.

She felt the pulsing of his cock as he came, her channel milking him as it squeezed and pulsed around him. They continued to move together slowly as they shuddered and twitched with zings of pleasure rolling through them.

When they finally stilled, Daniel released Devlin's wrist and withdrew from her. The cold air rushed in as he rolled off her body, trekking across her sensitive skin in a way that was almost painful. She heard Daniel moving a bit beside her, and then, suddenly, he was there with a blanket he drew over both of them. He reached for her arm, still resting on the bed above her head, and gently took her hand. He drew it to his lips and kissed her palm.

Devlin turned to look at him in all his disheveled glory. "That was..." She trailed off, not sure how to describe something as epic as what had just gone down in that bed.

"Agreed," Daniel replied as he leaned in to kiss her gently on the lips. "You are something special. I've never felt..." He just shook his head, at a loss.

Devlin chuckled. "So I guess that means this was a date?"

"I think it's pretty safe to say!" He snorted. "Is it too late for me to be a gentleman and get you that drink?" He had an amused twinkle in his eye.

"The shit is already out of the horse, but I suppose I can cut you some slack." Devlin gave him a cheeky wink. "This time..."

CHAPTER TWENTY-ONE

Devlin sat, propped against the pillows in bed, watching Daniel throw on a pair of jogging pants. *Hottie McBody!* She tipped her face up as he leaned down and dropped a kiss on her lips.

"I'm going to check what we have in the bar. I haven't gotten into it since I've been back." He gave her a wink as he headed into the large, open living room.

"I'll be there in a minute." Devlin eyed her clothes that littered the floor.

Not a chance in Hell. The idea of putting on dress pants, no matter how comfy, didn't appeal to her in the least. *Aha!* Daniel's button-down shirt was on the floor near the foot of the bed. She stretched out her arm, and the shirt lifted off the floor, zipping through the air directly into her open hand. *Error 404 File Not Found.* Devlin sat there stunned. Her brain was glitching, trying to reconcile what had just happened. She was scrambling, trying to convince herself that she was imagining things but flashing through the weird occurrences of the past few days. *Hot flashes, red eyes, radio glitches, unidentified flying shirts... Lions and tigers and bears, oh my!*

When she was young, her dad had prepared her for what the manifestation of power would be like. At thirty, without a hint of magic making an appearance, they had both assumed it wasn't going to happen. Devlin had accepted that she would live a normal, mortal life. Her heart was racing in sheer panic. Sticking her head in the sand, enacting an Ostrich Protocol, seemed like the best path forward.

Blessedly, Daniel interrupted her mental spiral by shouting from the other room. "What's your poison?"

Devlin stuttered as the here-and-now came crashing back in. "Um, yeah... I'll take a gin and tonic," she shouted back as she stared at the shirt she had crushed in her fist. "I'll be right out!"

Ostrich Protocol engaged! Devlin threw off the blanket and swung her legs over the edge of the bed as she slipped into Daniel's dress shirt. The shirt fell to mid-thigh. She took a steadying breath, walked over to the wall, and flicked on the light. The sudden brightness had her blinking hard. Slightly terrified of what she would see, Devlin took the few steps over to the dresser. *Holy hideous harpies!* Her hair was a disaster of epic proportions. It looked like she had tried for an eighties' masterpiece but gave up halfway through! No red eyes, horns, or a tail. She'd take the hair-tastrophe any day of the week! Devlin frantically searched the dresser for a brush, to no avail. With no other choice, she finger-combed it as quickly as she could. *That's as good as it's going to get.* She shrugged at her reflection, took a deep breath, and walked out of the bedroom.

Daniel was standing at a small bar-top cabinet pouring tonic water from a can into a rocks glass. He turned to look at her and locked in, eyeing her up and down so hungrily it stopped her in her tracks.

"Shit! Fuck!" Daniel shouted as tonic water overflowed the glass.

Devlin laughed out loud. This was just what the doctor ordered to chase away the worst of the panic hovering the edge of every moment. Still chuckling, she headed over to help Daniel wipe the fizzy mess off the table.

"I hope this is okay." she motioned to the shirt she'd stolen.

Daniel looked at her with heat in his eyes and ran his index finger from the base of her throat to the top of the first fastened button, just above her breasts. "Feel free to wear all of my shirts, anytime."

Devlin shivered, her body reacting to the heat in Daniel's gaze. His finger left an electric tingle in its wake.

"I guess I should just go shopping in your closet then," she whispered.

"Be my guest." Daniel leaned in to kiss her gently. Their lips clung, neither of them wanting to end the moment.

"I swear this isn't what I was trying for when I invited you out tonight," Daniel murmured.

Devlin shifted slightly to drop a trail of kisses from Daniel's lips down to the base of his throat. He made a small noise of appreciation.

She gave his neck a little lick and nip before replying. "It wasn't on my agenda either, but I'm not going to complain."

"Damn right," Daniel breathed.

Devlin tucked herself more closely into Daniel's warmth.

"You must be freezing," Daniel said as he began fussing over her.

He led her to the couch, pulling a large tartan throw blanket off the back. He motioned for her to sit and draped the blanket around her shoulders. Daniel returned to the bar and got her drink, bringing it over, and setting it down on the coffee table in front of her.

"One gin and tonic," he said with a flourish of presentation. "Now, time to get a fire going." He turned to the large stone fireplace with purpose.

Devlin had to keep reminding herself not to drool as she watched Daniel build the fire. While he stacked the logs, she couldn't help but wonder if he'd cut them himself. Her imagination began to wander as she watched the muscles of his back ripple as he moved the wood into place. Images of Daniel, shirtless, swinging an axe, ran through her mind as she lifted the gin and tonic to her lips. Devlin's thoughts turned to all the farm work Daniel must have done in his time. Baling hay at Joe's farm would sure have been a hell of a lot more enjoyable if he'd Magic Mike'd it and stripped down. *New drinking game… For every naughty thought, take a drink!* Devlin rolled her eyes and shook her head. *Death by alcohol poisoning, one hundred percent!*

"What's up?" Daniel asked as he sank down onto the couch beside her.

"Oh, nothing." Devlin gave him a guilty smile.

Daniel picked up his own drink and swirled the amber liquid in his glass. He looked like he was pondering something intense. Not wanting to disturb him, Devlin turned to watch the fire. She was entranced by the dangerous, hypnotic beauty of the flames as they danced. The fire was somehow calming. The echoes of her earlier panic slid farther away as the flames licked higher and higher. She could hear Daniel saying something, but it sounded far away. Devlin was fixated; she couldn't make her brain shift focus. The flames were as high as the opening of the fireplace, their brightly burning tongues licking over the edge.

Suddenly Daniel was there, shifting logs around

with the fireplace poker.

"Damn it, I must have put too many logs in. Those flames were getting crazy!"

Devlin blinked, her brain coming back on-line. "Oh, wow. Is it going to be okay?"

Daniel took a relieved breath and put the poker back in its place. "It looks like it."

Devlin's stomach flipped as the flames dropped down to their original levels almost instantly. *Shit, shit shit... That was you, dumbass.* Panic popped up again to say hello. How was this going to affect her life? Was she a danger to those around her? She needed to get off her ass and call her dad but didn't want to leave the normalcy of Daniel's couch. If she made that call, her life would never be the same.

Daniel was a very hot anchor that she wanted to stay tied to. His strong arms wrapped around her, drawing her into his warm, comforting body. It was like he had felt her anxiety and reacted instinctively. He took her glass and placed it on the table, tucking her more closely against him. There were no questions. He wasn't looking for an explanation for her sudden shift in mood. He just held her, absently rubbing the pad of his thumb soothingly against her arm as they rested together.

She wasn't sure how much time passed, but Devlin felt her panic fade back to a niggling worry. She shifted slightly to look up at Daniel's face. That pensive look had made a return visit. Devlin desperately wanted to know what was occupying his thoughts, and lucky for her, she didn't have to wait long to find out.

"You impressed me from day one, you know." Daniel looked down to meet her eyes. He gave her a crooked smile and a helpless shrug at her look of shock and incredulity. "It's true. I'd never seen anybody write such a beautiful contract. You have such a thorough understanding of the law. It's hot. Then I saw you at your office, and I couldn't imagine someone so brilliant *and* beautiful."

Devlin shifted off his chest to look him full in the face. "Really?"

He chuckled ruefully. "You have no idea how frustrating it was to want you so badly. It felt like a betrayal of my father's legacy. To my embarrassment, I figured it would be easier to make you hate me."

"You sure did a good job convincing me." Devlin poked him in the arm. "To be fair, I thought you were pretty hot too, even when you were busy hijacking my office like a douche."

Daniel's face scrunched at the memory. "Yeah... you were pretty pissed." He shifted a bit uncomfortably, running his hand through his hair and rubbing his chin. "I haven't exactly been a 'lucky in love' kind of guy. You're just... You're extraordinary." He swallowed nervously, searching her face.

It was the uncertainty and vulnerability in his eyes that did it. Devlin didn't even try to hold herself back. She slid one hand up to cup his cheek. There was no hope of explaining how she felt. Words were not going to cut it at the moment; the only solution was to show him. Daniel must have felt the same way. They moved toward each other like magnets, their lips meeting softly, but that didn't last long. The sensation of his skin beneath her palm and his lips against hers had Devlin melting into him. Her tongue slipped out to run along the seam of his lips, and he opened his mouth to welcome her in.

They dueled for supremacy, with Daniel ultimately plundering her mouth with his. His hands landed on her body, one around the back of her neck, the other sliding around her waist as he tried to draw her closer. Their position on the couch just wasn't working for them. Devlin slid back, reaching out to Daniel, wanting to stretch out together. His eyes darted around the room. With a cheeky smile, he cocked his head toward the fire, holding out a hand to draw Devlin to her feet.

Moments later, she was lying on the soft rug in front of the fire as Daniel raced back from the bedroom, condom in hand. He tossed it on the floor and stretched out beside her.

"Better?" he murmured as he nuzzled her neck.

Devlin practically purred her response. "Much."

She slid her hand down Daniel's chest, his muscles twitching slightly as she traveled lower and lower. She toyed with the waistband of his joggers, slipping her finger under the elastic and sliding it slowly back and forth across his skin. He sucked in a ragged breath as she teased him.

"Payback's a cold, hard bitch," she said, giving him a wicked look as she slid her hand into his pants and grasped his cock. "Definitely hard," she said with a naughty wink.

Daniel made a valiant effort to distract her so he could take the lead, but Devlin was having none of it. She rolled him onto his back, straddling his legs to hold him at her mercy. In an echo of their earlier activities, she took his wrists and drew them up to place them on the floor above his head.

"Keep those still," she said as she dragged one of her nails from his shoulder, down the centre of his chest, past his belly button, and along the bulge of his cock as it twitched at her touch.

One of Daniel's arms lifted off the floor to reach out for her, and she batted it away.

"Put that back, or I'll stop." She gave him a stern teacherly look.

The arm went straight back to its place on the floor. "Yes, ma'am."

Daniel clasped his hands together in a bid to keep them from moving again. His eyes glittered with anticipation.

Devlin hovered over him, nipping his chin then leaning down to drag her tongue down the path her finger had taken. She moved slowly, watching as Daniel's chest rose and fell more rapidly. When she reached his waist, she grasped his pants and drew them over his hips, sliding them down to his knees. The flag pole was ready for action the moment it was freed.

"We'll just leave those there for now." She kissed her way back up one thigh, skimming her nails up the other.

Devlin smiled with a touch of evil. She felt powerful having him at her mercy. She held Daniel's gaze as her tongue snaked out to lick the length of his cock. She blew gently on the tip, making it pulse in anticipation.

"Please," he begged.

Devlin just smiled and went back to playing with her new toy. Her tongue circled around the crown as she dug her nails into his ass to hold him still. She heard him groan. *Payback, baby.* She smiled with satisfaction at the success of her slow torture. She gave him another thorough lick then slid his length into her mouth. She grasped the base of his cock as she began swirling her tongue while she sucked on him. Daniel's hips moved of their own accord, beginning a gentle thrust and retreat. She looked up to take in his face. It was a mask of pleasure. His eyes were wild, and his whole body was vibrating with the strain of holding his arms still.

"Please!" Daniel cried again with more urgency.

Devlin felt him growing harder and harder. She knew he wouldn't last much longer if she kept teasing him with her mouth. She raised her head, and his cock left her mouth with a *pop*. She spied the shiny condom wrapper and reached out to grab it. Blessedly the condom didn't magically appear in her hand. Devlin quite happily leaned over and snatched it off the floor. She ripped it open and rolled it slowly over his shaft.

"Can I touch you now?" Daniel pleaded as he watched her shimmy up his legs to position herself.

Devlin pretended to give it some thought. "Hmmmm…nope!"

She smiled and reached down to hold him steady as she rubbed him between her folds, back and forth. She felt the pulsing of her own swollen channel. She held his cock at her entrance and slid down slowly. Her body clenched and released around him as he filled her. They both groaned as she buried him in her body to the hilt, bearing down as hard as she could.

Devlin slowly undid the buttons of her shirt, letting it fall open slowly to reveal her breasts. She slid the shirt off her arms and tossed it onto the couch.

Daniel made tortured sounds as he struggled to keep his arms above his head as he'd been told.

"I'm sure you've noticed I can be a bit of a control freak too," she said in a breathy voice.

Her inner muscles clenched as she lifted herself up and sank back down. Devlin grasped her breasts as she rode him, teasing and pinching her nipples as she slid up and down on his cock. Daniel's hips pumped as he matched her rhythm. One hand slipped down her body to her clit as the other continued teasing her breast. Daniel let out a strangled sound as he watched her hand slide between her legs as she rode him. Her fingers danced over slick flesh, rubbing her clit and caressing her opening as Daniel stretched her with his cock. Her other hand left her breast, moving down to spread her lips open, giving Daniel a better view. His hips jacked up wildly, pistoning faster and more erratically. Devlin felt him twitch inside her, and her body responded in kind, tightening and pulsing. She felt that same full-body tingle she'd felt before. Her fingers flew, rubbing her clit faster and faster as "little Daniel" massaged the most delicious spot over and over until she cried out. The explosion took her breath away.

Devlin's release was so powerful she heard ringing in her ears. She watched Daniel's face as he screamed her name. She felt his cock kicking inside her as she wrung him dry. Devlin's blood raced through her body as she collapsed on Daniel's chest. His arms finally moved to encircle her, holding her close.

CHAPTER TWENTY-TWO

Devlin stretched out her arm and frowned as her fingers touched something hard and cold. Cracking one eye open, she realized that she was lying on the rug and the cold hard thing was the stone fireplace. The fire had burned itself out at some point during the night. The harsh morning light streamed in through the cabin's large windows. She pulled the plaid blanket up over her head. *Oh goody, naked as a jaybird.* Devlin sighed as she pondered how frightful she must look.

Clanking noises and an amazing smell from the kitchen area made her curious. She pulled the blanket down just below her nose and snuck a peek across the open-concept living space. Daniel was mucking about in the kitchen with pots and pans. Devlin realized she was smelling eggs, pancakes, and freshly brewed coffee. Her stomach growled. *He cooks too!*

She peeked around the living room area, keeping the blanket pulled up as high as she could. Devlin desperately tried to remember where she'd tossed her shirt the night before. A flash of white against the dark

145

material of the couch caught her attention. *It couldn't have been nearby, right?* She darted a glance back toward the kitchen. Daniel seemed pretty focused on flipping pancakes, but she'd still have to get this done as quietly as a mouse. No need for him to see her looking like she'd been dragged through a hedge backward…naked. Devlin got on all fours, her head mostly covered by the blanket as she crawled as quiet as the grave toward the couch. She shot hasty glances toward the kitchen, making sure Daniel was still preoccupied. *Duh, Duh, duh-duh, Duh, Duh, duh-duh, Dah-di-dooooo, Dah-di-dooooo.* The *Mission Impossible* theme song echoed in her head as she snuck silently over to the couch. She slowly, quietly reached out to retrieve her shirt. New problem. There was no way she'd be able to get past Daniel to the bedroom without being spotted. She would have to find a way to sort herself out here, in the wild.

Devlin kept the blanket draped over her as she shimmied into the shirt, buttoning it up and pulling it down over her naked butt. She slipped her head out and dragged her fingers through her hair quickly to take care of the most horrifying knots. *Shit, teeth!* She lifted a cupped hand to cover her nose and mouth and did a quick breath-check. *Not horrible, but not spectacular either.* Devlin prayed to Leviathan that Daniel's family were mint-dish types. She slipped out from under the blanket and slunk along the floor, hugging the wall and reaching up to feel around inside any dishes she saw. *Bingo! Dish number three!* Her fingers closed over the crinkly candy wrapper as gently as possible to avoid making noise. It looked like an after-dinner mint that restaurants gave out with the bill at the end of a meal. She unwrapped it and popped it into her mouth. With a silent apology to her dentist, Devlin bit down on the mint to break it up, chewing fast so she could start acting like a normal human being sooner rather than later.

Once she was satisfied that her breath wouldn't make Daniel drop dead, she stood up and walked as nonchalantly as possible into the kitchen area. In reality, her heart was pounding and her legs were shaking. It wasn't like her to be this shy and nervous, but it seemed to be her new reality. She slipped onto a bar stool at the island between the kitchen and the living room. Daniel had his back to her as he manned the stove. *It should be illegal for that man to be shirtless.* Devlin was itching to reach out and touch him. The easy way they'd talked at lunch, the fun they'd had skating, and the insane sexual connection between them had her shook. She'd never experienced anything like this, and truthfully, it was scary and overwhelming.

A plate of food appeared in front of her, followed by a piping-hot cup of coffee. Daniel cupped her face in his palm and kissed her gently. Devlin breathed in soap and a touch of cologne.

Daniel shook his head. "You have been the most unexpected, maddeningly brilliant, gorgeous surprise!"

Devlin's heart simultaneously flipped and melted. "You're not so bad yourself." She smiled coyly. "I can honestly say I've never had such an…explosive evening."

"I thought you were going to kill me last night. I haven't come that hard in my life." Daniel's eyes dilated as he thought back to their evening. "What a way to go! You can boss me around whenever you want." He winked.

"I could say the same to you." Devlin reached out to touch his arm. "I'm not sure what this is, but it's something I want more of. *You're* something I want more of."

"Well, that's a relief!" Daniel exhaled with a laugh.

"Right?"

"So"—Daniel turned to put his dishes in the sink — "I have a couple more meetings today, but I'd love to grab a late lunch with you, if you're up for it."

Those damn butterflies starting flapping around inside her again. "Sounds great!"

"Excellent!" Daniel gave her another quick kiss and headed toward the bedroom. He continued to talk to her through the semi-open door. "There are fresh towels in the bathroom, and you can use my toothbrush if you want. I'll leave you my car keys so you can get wherever you want to go today. The spare cabin key is in the cookie jar beside the sink." He emerged from the bedroom, tucking a dress shirt into a fresh pair of pants. The top button of his shirt was open, and a tie was hanging loosely around his neck.

"Thank you for the offer, but you should take your car. I have no idea where we are, so text me the street address and I'll order an Uber." She walked over to Daniel and reached up to slip his shirt button into its home. "I *will* happily take a shower though." She slipped his tie into place, made sure it was straight, and smoothed it down his chest.

"I'm off!" Daniel grabbed his winter jacket and shrugged it on.

Before he walked out the door, Daniel turned to look at Devlin one more time. It was a look full of possibility. Then, with a wink, he was gone.

She stood rooted to the spot, marveling at how nice it had felt to wake up with Daniel. It had felt right to kiss him and send him off for the day. The only thing missing was a trip to her own office. Devlin had never been with anyone who had remotely tempted her to ponder a future of coupledom. Not until the infuriating Daniel Webster. She mulled this over as she headed into the kitchen and took the top off the cookie jar. The cabin key was right where he said it would be. She picked it up and turned it over in her hand. This all felt *very* real.

The sound of her ringtone caught her by surprise. She'd been out of contact with everyone at home since before they'd gone skating. It had to be a personal best for device avoidance. She ran to the front hall and dug around her in coat pockets until her hand closed around her phone. Her dad's photo flashed on the screen. *This should be interesting.*

She slid her finger across the screen and hit the speaker icon. "Hi, Dad." She tried to sound as normal as possible.

"Hi, my girl, how are things going in the Great White North?"

The muffled sounds of traffic in the background told her he was calling from his town car.

She walked into the bedroom as she spoke. "I'm good. I actually wanted to talk to you about drawing out the timing of the sale." She set her phone down on the dresser and picked up the hairbrush Daniel had left out for her.

"What about the timing?" Her dad sounded confused for good reason. It wasn't like her to ask for an extension on anything.

She winced as she drew the brush through a hunk of her hair, hitting a mountain of knots. "I've spent some time with Daniel Webster, and I think it's fair to give him a day or two to come up with a purchase plan.

He'd like to try making an offer to his siblings."

"Fair...?" Damien's voice dripped with skepticism as he waited her for to explain.

"You know, because it was his father's legacy." Devlin swallowed nervously as she replied, marveling at how her dad always managed to make her feel like a child when she was skirting an issue.

"Of course," he replied indulgently.

Devlin could still hear a touch of suspicion in his voice.

"I'll give you an update later today." She put the brush down and picked up her phone.

There was no point in delaying the inevitable. Devlin knew she had to pull her head out of her ass and deal with reality. *Big girl pants on.* She walked over to the bed and plopped down, leaning against the pillows and crossing her legs. She felt like a kid that needed her dad to comfort her.

"Dad..."

"Yes, my girl?" His velvety smooth voice floated down the line.

She took a deep breath and went for it. "Something's happening to me." She picked at the bedspread nervously. "I've been having some issues with...well...telekinesis...or pyrokinesis... some kind of 'esis.' I don't know what it is, but I've basically turned into a beacon for weirdness."

The line went eerily silent for a moment, and then Damien spoke. "What *exactly* has been happening?" He maintained a carefully measured tone.

"Um, well…a bit of radio interference, extreme hot flashes that make me dread menopause, a bad case of red-eye, shattering glassware, exploding lighting, and a touch of near-arson thrown in for good measure." She winced as she rattled it all off out loud for the first time. *Damn.*

Damien sighed. "We knew this could happen. I had written it off at this stage, but here we are…"

"Dad?"

"Sorry, my girl. I'm waging a bit of an internal war here. Part of me is sad you'll have to adjust to changes. The other part of me is thrilled that you'll be able to finally explore this huge part of your heritage… Limbo…the whole realm!" Devlin could tell her dad was trying hard to tamp down his excitement. "At the end of the day, it doesn't really matter how I feel. What matters is how *you* feel."

"I don't know." Devlin swallowed hard. "I'm scared that I'll accidentally hurt someone. I don't want to leave Da…North Bay, just yet. Is there anything I can do to keep this under wraps for a few more days? I'm not sure what to do." Devlin closed her eyes, hoping her dad hadn't caught her near slip-up but praying to Cerberus he could give her a Band-Aid for this bullet hole.

"It sounds like North Bay has really grown on you," Damien replied as Devlin face-palmed herself for being such a crappy actor. He'd seen right through that one. "I would suggest you come home as soon as you can, though. You'll need training to manage your magic. It will only get more volatile the longer you wait."

"It should only be a couple of days." Devlin felt a bit better now that she'd had a chance to chat with her dad. "I love you."

"I love you, too, my girl. Just be cautious. We haven't identified the catalyst for your evolution. I would stay out of crowded, public places to be on the safe side."

"I will, I promise. Love you, Dad." She hung up and tossed her phone onto the bed.

Devlin went back to the mirror and picked up the hairbrush, charging back into battle with her knots. She made a valiant attempt to lock her worries away in a tiny mental box, to be examined later. She was determined to have a couple more days with Daniel before reality reared its ugly head, and she didn't intend to waste them.

CHAPTER TWENTY-THREE

Devlin was flying high. She was walking on a cloud at the shop as she picked up her rental car. She drove back to the hotel on auto-pilot; her thoughts were full of Daniel. Their connection felt like a once-in-a-lifetime sort of thing. She'd have to head back to Toronto sooner rather than later, but she was going to Marie Kondo the shit out of the next couple of days. Daniel *definitely* sparked joy! Despite the many question marks around her magic, Devlin was going to think positively. Her dad managed a pretty normal life—by mortal standards—so why shouldn't she expect the same?

Her bubble burst when she finally sat down on her hotel bed and fired up her laptop. The number of unread items in her inbox was better than a bucket of ice water to shock her back to reality. Devlin normally enjoyed her work, but at the moment, this did *not* spark joy, that was for damn sure. What a shame she couldn't just delete them! There were no less than half a dozen emails from Kitty, with updates and amendments on several outstanding contracts, a slew of requests to return missed phone calls, and a handful of emails marked *urgent* about Harvest Time. Devlin twisted a lock of hair around her finger as she stared at the flagged messages. She wasn't the type of person to shy away from difficult situations, but she just didn't have it in her to deal with Daniel's highly objectionable siblings just yet. She unwound the hair from her finger and flipped it over her shoulder with a sigh. *It's not procrastinating. It's proactively delaying.*

Instead of diving into the other work she had piling up like a digital Mount Everest, Devlin went back to daydreaming about Daniel. Her brain was serving her visions of visiting him in North Bay, of him making trips to Toronto, spending time at each other's favorite places. They could have an endless stream of nights like the last and wake up together the next day to do it all over again.

She flicked the lid of her laptop closed and fell back on the bed to stare at the ceiling. It was ridiculous to be thinking like this after one amazing night, but she had this overwhelming, stomach-flipping, heart-pounding, blood-rushing need for Daniel. She was riding an oxytocin high, and she knew it! *Hey, Universe! Spec-fucking-tacular timing!* Devlin had dated her fair share of guys, but it had always felt a bit superficial. She was basically going through the motions. There was nothing *wrong* with them. They just didn't stir anything in her. She had finally met someone that challenged her *and* made her body burn, *just* in time to start turning into a movie villain. *Devlin Laflamme, Destructo-Girl!*

With a reluctant groan, Devlin picked up her mobile and dialed Kitty. Time to adult and get some work done. She dragged herself upright just as the phone rang.

"Boss! I was about to send a search party for you!" Kitty sounded so relieved to hear from her it buried the needle on Devlin's guilt-o-meter.

"Kitty, I'm sorry. I got so side-tracked up here that I've let everything slip." She knew how pathetic the excuse sounded, and she felt like an ass for making Kitty worry.

"You're forgiven, but you have to fill me in on everything that's happened! It must have been epic to keep you this tied up!" Kitty, forever the forgiving soul, just swept it under the rug, and Devlin was thankful. "I've sent you some updates on our other deals. There are two that are finalized that need your signature and one with new red-lines to review."

"Thank you so much, Kitty. You really are the best. I'd lose my head if you weren't there to help keep it screwed on." She hoped Kitty understood how much she meant it. They'd been through the corporate trenches together, and Devlin couldn't imagine wading through that wasteland with anyone else.

"Oh, and there was urgent matter that Mister

Laflamme took care of for Harvest Time. I emailed you an updated file. He said he'd give you a call later to walk you through the details. He'll be in meetings until around three o'clock." Devlin heard Kitty clicking away on her keyboard.

She frowned in confusion. "What urgent matter?"

"I didn't read through the details, since Mr. Laflamme took care of it personally. He said that you shouldn't worry about it and that he'd call you tonight." Devlin could practically hear Kitty's shrug.

"Okay, well, since Dad took care of it, I guess that buys me time to review the other files on the docket. Fun times!" Devlin joked.

"Nah." Kitty chuckled. "You're always working crazy hours. Why don't you just take some time for yourself! Relax, watch TV, read a book, go to a spa!"

A day of relaxation couldn't go wrong. She hadn't taken time off work in ages, so why the hell not! "You know what. I think you're right."

"Good!" Kitty sounded way too happy, and it made Devlin wonder if she should be questioning her life choices.

"Gotta fly. The other line's ringing! Call me if you need me!" With that, Kitty was gone.

Devlin shook her head in amusement. Kitty was full of energy, and she wouldn't have it any other way. She was tempted to turn her laptop back on to read the

Harvest Time update email but managed to talk herself down. It would keep until later. Devlin knew she really did need to find a better work-life balance. Kitty usually stuck with thinly veiled hints about taking time off, but she had clearly graduated to bashing Devlin over the head with it!

Her phone dinged, and Daniel's name popped up on the screen. Devlin's heart skipped a beat as she opened the message. She read it and smiled. Daniel wanted to meet up earlier than they had planned. Her hands were shaking with excitement as she tapped out a suggestion to meet at Diane's café. Her heart flipped when Daniel responded in the affirmative. *Coffee and a muffin…a stud-muffin that is! Sweet!*

CHAPTER TWENTY-FOUR

On the walk to Diane's café, Devlin was smiling so hard her face was hurting. The rest of her personal paranormal melodrama would still be waiting for her later. Right now, she just wanted to see Daniel's face and hear about his day. Devlin hadn't read that Harvest Time update email from Kitty, but she hoped it had something to do with Daniel's buy-out efforts. Maybe he'd had some success in finding an investor!

As she approached the café, she could see that Daniel had beaten here there. He was sitting at the table she'd shared with Diane, looking lost in thought. Devlin smiled and waved as she opened the door. It was oddly quiet as she headed toward the table. Daniel remained still, staring down at his coffee. She turned to say a quick hello to Diane but stopped short when she saw the stony expression on Diane's face. *What the actual fuck?*

When she got to the table, Daniel didn't get up, he didn't hug her, in fact he didn't even look at her. This was a complete one-eighty from the Daniel she'd parted with just that morning in the cabin. Devlin shrugged out of her coat, hung it over the back of her chair, and sat down.

"Is everything okay?" Devlin asked in confusion as Daniel finally lifted his eyes to meet hers. If looks could kill, Devlin would have met a gruesome demise.

"What do you think?" Daniel spat out; his words dripped with contempt.

"Well, I'm going out on a limb to say something's definitely wrong." Devlin was baffled by this turn of events.

Daniel made a derisive noise. "You're damn right there's something wrong," he scoffed as he narrowed his eyes at her. "So, is this your standard move when someone isn't falling in line with what you want?"

Devlin leaned back in her seat, putting a bit of much-needed distance between herself and the stranger across from her. "What on earth are you talking about?"

"Does daddy send you in to screw the unsuspecting idiot to distract him, while he goes behind their back to fuck them in a deal?" Daniel made sound of disgust. "What a hellish pair you are. Your father has a reputation for driving hard deals. I guess the poisoned apple doesn't fall far from the tree."

Oh hell no! Devlin felt her blood start boiling. "Let me stop you right there," she began but stopped short when Daniel made a cutting motion and spoke over her.

"You know what. It's my fault for being so stupid and trusting. I took my eye off the ball. I should have seen this coming." He stood and swung his coat on in one smooth move. "I never want to speak to you or see you ever again," he said as he fished in his wallet and pulled out a twenty, tossing it onto the table. "Here. Coffee's on me. Consider it part of your spoils."

Daniel stepped around the table and marched out the door without another word or a backward glance. Devlin sat there alone in a state of shock. To put a cherry on top of this clusterfuck pie, Diane walked over and picked up the cash.

"I warned you about hurting him. He's already been through enough." She gave Devlin a withering glare before walking away with one last, delightful parting message. "Don't let the door hit you in the ass on your way out."

Devlin was fuming as she put her jacket on and headed toward the café door. There *was* one thing she knew for certain. She wouldn't talk to Daniel Webster ever again. Not until all the realms of Hell had frozen over and demons were having princess tea parties in fancy dress!

Diane shrieked from behind the counter as the lights inside the café exploded in their fixtures. Sparks rained down as Devlin stepped out into the street.

CHAPTER TWENTY-FIVE

Devlin went back to the hotel, packed her stuff, and checked out in record time. She wanted to put as many kilometers as she could between herself and North Bay... *and* Daniel, as fast as possible. Back in Toronto, Devlin just felt drained. All of her piss and vinegar had slid away during the long drive home. She was going through the motions, and it hadn't gone unnoticed, particularly by the ever-observant Kitty, who hovered outside her office door like a helicopter. Devlin just didn't have the bandwidth to deal with any fuckery from anyone. She'd dragged her sorry ass in and closed her office door firmly behind her.

She was sitting in her chair, slowly spinning it around and around, when her door swung open, banging against the wall. Damien stepped in with a flourish, like a magician about to do a big reveal. The smile disappeared from his face the moment he got a good look at her.

"What's wrong, sweetheart?" he asked as he swung the door closed to give them privacy.

Devlin put her elbows on her desk and rested her chin on her fists. "I don't wanna talk about it." She knew she sounded like a moody teenager, but that was, quite frankly, exactly how she felt.

Damien took the seat in front of her desk and plopped a huge antique book down on its surface with a thud. "Does this have anything to do with Daniel Webster?" he asked softly.

She didn't have to say a word; her face did all the work. Damien sighed then shook his head in confusion. "I had a feeling something was going on. You've never been good at hiding things from me, my girl." He gave her a sympathetic smile. "What happened? I thought you'd *both* be happy now that everything's sorted out with the business."

Devlin frowned. "What do you mean? Sorted out? Did Daniel find an investor in time to make a deal?" Hope for Daniel's quest to save his family legacy warred with her hurt and anger.

"I had Kitty send you an update when the sale closed. You didn't read it?" Damien sounded puzzled, not accustomed to Devlin leaving items unread.

"No, I had a…personal issue…yesterday, and I haven't gotten around to it yet." She was having *all* the feelings and was barely managing to keep them from spewing out into the world.

The fluorescent overhead lighting started to

flicker.

"I was going to go through the fine print with you yesterday, but you didn't answer when I called." Damien pointed toward her laptop. "Why don't we go through it now?"

Devlin powered on her laptop and logged into her email account as Damien picked up his chair and moved it around the desk. He plunked it down beside her and leaned in *very* cautiously, like he was afraid she might bite. Devlin clicked open the file attached to Kitty's email.

"Scroll to page four." Damien glanced over his shoulder at Devlin's printer, which had suddenly sprung to life, pulling paper from the paper tray and spitting it out all over the floor.

Devlin didn't react to the minor technological meltdown; she was too busy searching the contract. There it was, about a third of the way down the page. Her dad had closed the sale of Harvest Time Garden Market. Not only had he closed it, he had paid considerably higher than market value.

"But why...?" She trailed off as she skimmed the rest of the document.

"Daniel's siblings weren't willing to wait the extra few days we'd asked for. They wanted to approach other firms to see if they could get competitive offers. I had a feeling after our last conversation that you and Daniel were...working well together...so I went in with a high offer to close it quickly. They used their majority vote to sign off on it right away." Damien frowned. "Didn't Daniel tell you any of this?"

"No...but now I understand why he was so hacked off. He wanted to save the business. A high sale price won't mean anything to him. It was about his father." Devlin dropped her head down and leaned her forehead against her desk. "He must have thought I knew about this. No wonder he thought...what he thought." She caught herself just in time. There was no point getting her dad wound up by letting slip that Daniel had insinuated he was using his own daughter for sexpionage. *Pussy Galore of the legal world, right here, folks!*

Damien shook his head and slid the laptop closer. "That doesn't make any sense." He scrolled to the final page of the sale agreement and pointed at a passage of the contract. "I told Daniel's brother that I was buying the business and putting it in your name. With the business registered to you, *you* can decide its fate. Keep it and run it or sell it to Daniel for a dollar. It's up to you."

Devlin was shocked. "Dad...that's...I don't know what to say." She leaned into him, hugging him tightly as tears burned her eyes. "Thank you for doing this."

"It sounds like Chad Webster may have withheld some vital information." Damien dropped a kiss on her forehead.

She nodded. "Daniel must think I bought the company out from under him for myself."

Damien smiled as he stood and headed toward the door. "Maybe it wouldn't hurt to give him a call. Talk it through?" He raised an eyebrow and leaned in, speaking in a stage whisper. "We need to talk about that other thing later. It will be hard to explain exploding light bulbs and widespread equipment outages to maintenance." He gave her a conspiratorial wink. "Oh, and you may want to give that a read." He pointed to the massive tome he'd left behind.

Devlin slid it across her desk to get a better look. Her dad had taught her Latin when she was young. It was a staple in the infernal education system, and her dad wanted to make sure she had a full education. How could one properly participate in an exorcism without it! She read the faded gilt lettering and raised an eyebrow at her dad.

"The Nephilim?" she asked. "You used to tell me bedtime fables about them when I was young." Devlin smiled at the happy memory.

Damien nodded. "They weren't just children's tales. I figured if you developed magical abilities, it would be less shocking if you were familiar with the lore."

"But Nephilim only exist in stories. They were

wiped from existence millennia ago."

"Until now," Damien said with a loving smile.

Devlin sat, stunned as the pieces of her strange life clicked together. She saw the complete puzzle for the first time. Her mother was human, and her dad, the Morningstar, was a fallen angel. She was the product of their union, making her...Nephil. She stared at her dad in open-mouthed shock.

Damien chuckled. "You're catching flies, my girl."

Devlin snapped her jaw closed, making her dad laugh out loud. "I suspect your magical incidents are tied to emotional triggers. We're going to have to get that under control *tout suite*! I'd rather not have to deal with a bunch of insurance claims that could be difficult to explain."

"Right..." Devlin nodded.

"It's important that *you* control your powers, not the other way around." Damien glanced down at his watch. "Shit! I have a meeting that's starting in five. I'll have Craig set up some time to work with you. He will be able to help with techniques for focus and control. I think it's best I leave this to a third-party. We all know how much fun we had when I tried to teach you how to drive. Best we not repeat that experience." The sarcasm was unmistakable.

They had fought like cats and dogs, ultimately

deciding that it would be much better for their relationship if she worked with a driving instructor. Devlin laughed and rolled her eyes. "True. But Craig? Your personal assistant?"

"Yes, dear. Craig is, in fact, an incubus…not that he exercises his special allure at work. That would be a lawsuit waiting to happen!"

Devlin's eyebrows crawled up her forehead as her dad blew her a kiss and disappeared from her doorway. *What a gong show of a day!*

CHAPTER TWENTY-SIX

Devlin had wasted the last *two days* trying to reach Daniel. She'd left message after message, with no response. The sliver of hope she'd held on to that they could deal with this colossal dumpster-fire of a misunderstanding had dwindled, then vanished. A sense of righteous indignation had taken its place. She sat on the leather sofa of her dad's study, her legs tucked up beside her, as she stared into her brandy. Damien had a late meeting, so their dinner had been reduced to drinks. Devlin wasn't a fan of being alone with her thoughts at the moment, so the wait was like death by a thousand paper cuts. Her dad's huge, empty wingback chair just reinforced the hollowness she felt inside. *Tick. Tick. Tick.* She was a grown woman but was always going to be a daddy's girl. Their relationship was unique. One part, dad-daughter, one part, friends.

Relief flooded through her as she heard her dad's voice booming from the front hallway. "Are you in the study, my girl?"

"Yup, in here, Dad." She placed her snifter on an

end table and got up to meet him as he made the grand entrance he could only make away from the eyes of mortals.

Damien materialized at the study door in a cloud of black smoke. Devlin didn't say a word. She just walked right up to him and wrapped her arms around him tight, laying her head over his heart.

Damien hugged her back with a deep sigh. "Oh, sweetheart…"

She squeezed him hard then stepped back with a sad smile. "I'll be fine I just need some company and a good bitching session."

"Then company you shall have!" Damien made a sweeping gesture, encompassing the entire study. "The realm of booze and bitching welcomes you. Enter at your peril, as I have just exited a meeting with the troglodyte who own the building I want to buy by the lake, and I, too, must bitch! That man is trying my patience in a way that makes me want to go medieval on his ass!"

Devlin laughed for the first time that day. Trust her dad's melodramatics to make her feel like the world was still spinning on its axis.

"The usual?" Devlin went to pour him a drink.

"But of course," Damien said as he took a seat in his chair.

No matter where he was, Damien always

managed to command the room with his regal presence. *You have to be pretty damned confident to start the most epic rebellion of all time!* Devlin handed her dad his snifter.

Damien eyed her over the rim of his glass as he took a sip of his drink. "Does the sour mood have anything to do with a certain Daniel Webster?"

"Of course not!" Devlin scoffed.

Her dad pursed his lips and raised an eyebrow.

"Ugh! I mean it's not like I want to have warm, fuzzy chats with him or anything. I just want him to know exactly how much of an ass-hat he's been. For the record, you know?"

"As you're well aware, I have no love for anyone that upsets you." Damien's expression darkened a tad. "but...I am willing to reach out to young Mister Webster if that's what you want. I hate seeing you upset like this, and if eviscerating him...with your words...will help, then I can get behind that." For just an instant, Damien's eyes flashed red. "I *could* do away with him though, if that's your preference. Just saying..."

"You're sweet, Dad, but no. If he can't even be bothered to return a call, then he isn't worth it." Devlin shrugged.

Damien looked thoughtful, nodding to himself as he nursed his drink.

Devlin's eyebrow rose. "Are you going to share with the class?"

"Smarty-pants." Damien winked. "Why don't you take some time off? Head to Limbo for a while. I can assign someone to run Harvest Time for you while you're away. You can have some time to yourself to clear your mind and test your magic in a liability-free zone."

"That may not be a bad idea." Devlin nodded slowly. "Now that I can actually get into the Underworld, I really *should* visit. It wouldn't do for the Devil's daughter not to make an appearance. Craig did mention it would be a good idea to train there. Less danger of being exposed to mortals." *Time to hop on the highway to Hell!*

"So, it's settled." Damien pounded his fist on the arm of his chair like a gavel.

"I heard a rumor that Daniel interviewed for an in-house counsel position at Voyager Industries."

Devlin and her dad had no love of that organization. They were constantly trying to poach Obsidian employees by offering ridiculously high salaries. Despite that, they had very little success.

"Best of luck to him." Damien raised his glass with a sarcastic chuckle. "Their company culture sucks donkey dick."

"I know. It's just…Daniel had to know I would hear about it. This is just one final 'fuck you' for the road." She puffed out a frustrated breath.

Damien shrugged. "They'll throw money at him,

but if he has half a brain, he'll see through it. Their employee turnover is bananas, and everyone in the industry knows it!"

Devlin pounded back the rest of her drink and winced. "Everyone has a price."

CHAPTER TWENTY-SEVEN

A vacation to the Underworld was exactly what the doctor ordered. Daily training sessions with Craig, her hot new incubus BFF, had proven to be both frustrating and fun. She hadn't been able to conjure up so much as a mouse fart of magic the entire time she'd been in Limbo. On the other hand, Craig was easy on the eyes, but more importantly, he was good people. She was starting to think of staying in the Underworld permanently. There had even been some talk of her helping with dispute arbitration between demonic legions. The only person who'd really miss her would be Kitty, and Devlin could always hop a portal to the mortal realm for a visit. Her fair-weather friends would replace her in a heartbeat. She'd never really gotten close to anyone. It was hard to have a best friend when you had to live a lie. Fun fact, people weren't too psyched to learn that Hell was real!

Devlin was staying at the family home in Limbo. She'd heard stories about it all her life, but nothing could have prepared her for the reality. The "family home" was a Baroque palace, with gilded trim and sumptuous draperies throughout. The throne room had a white marble floor with a red runner going all the way from the doorway to the dais, where a single throne with gilded arms and red upholstery sat in state. Her dad had an appreciation of the finer things. *That* was evident in the many antique treasures on display. Devlin suspected her dear old dad had a bad case of sticky fingers, since a lot of his prized possessions seemed to be "missing" from the mortal realm. The family home in Toronto had always felt a bit too big and showy, but now she could see how much her dad had reined it in. This place screamed Damien Laflamme...or Lucifer Morningstar... or The Lightbringer...or Satan...or the Devil...or...well, you take your pick! It was all a bit ostentatious for Devlin, but it was absolutely fitting for the Prince of Hell.

Her dad had told her stories about the many provinces and legions that inhabited the Underworld when she was a child. Limbo, the capital city, was a mashup of modern city living and old-world charm. Apartment buildings rose up from gaslit, cobbled streets. The sky was in a perpetual state of falling twilight. It was actually quite atmospheric. There were several portals between the Underworld and the mortal realm, but the main transit hub was set in the center of Limbo near the palace. Demons came and went, commuting between the realms. The city was laid out like a spiderweb that spread out far and wide, but all roads led to the Devil…her dad.

Devlin stood at a drawing room window, staring out at her kingdom. It was still hard to think of herself as a "royal," but the palace staff hadn't exactly given her much choice. Her dad's butler had taken to her quickly but was constantly tutting at her desire to do things for herself.

Vehicles drove down the lamp lit streets, demons milled about, shopping and running errands. It all seemed so normal. If you squinted, and didn't look too closely, it was easy to ignore the horns or tails or scales or fur. In the distance, smoke rose from behind the thick Roman walls surrounding the city. She could barely make out a thin stone bridge leading across a smoldering expanse. That bridge ended at their other, more forbidding "family home." *That* castle was a goth's wet dream, complete with gargoyles and heavy iron gates. It sat in the middle of a burning oil slick. Black smoke rose up and swirled around the building, occasionally obscuring it from view. She was *not* planning on spending much time at the "lake house," as her dad affectionately called it. Devlin had gotten good at distracting herself at this point. She could go hours feeling fine, and then, without warning, she'd think of *him* and be right back where she started.

"Enjoying the view?" Damien entered the room

with his typical swagger.

"It's really something," she said, turning to face him. "There's so much I need to learn," she mused.

Damien joined his daughter at the window. "True, but there's no rush. You can live a full life in the mortal realm then return. The Underworld isn't going anywhere."

"I want to stay."

"No need to rush into anything, my girl. I don't want you to miss out on something you'll regret."

Devlin turned to look into her dad's eyes. "Dad...?"

"It's just..." Damien rubbed the back of his neck, avoiding his daughter's gaze. "Daniel came to the office the other day looking for you."

Devlin's heart clenched, but she refused to show it. "Oh. Well, good for him."

"He said he couldn't stay away." Damien looked mega-guilty. "I *may* have disabused him of his erroneous assumptions about the business purchase."

"And?" *Enhance your calm, John Spartan.*

Damien turned to face her fully and cupped her cheek. "He realized he fucked up. He came all the way to the office *before* I told him anything. You know there's no way in...well, Hell, that I'd advocate for him if I'd sensed any deception."

Devlin laid her hand over her dad's. "Dad, you

know I love you, but I really need to you stay out of this one. Sometimes it's just too late to walk back stuff that's been said."

"You're stubborn, just like your mother," Damien said with a wistful smile. "I'm afraid I've done you a terrible disservice by not telling you more about her. It's just so painful to remember."

This was the one topic that had always been off the table, despite their closeness. "What about her?"

He clasped both of her hands in his as sadness washed over his face. "I never thought I'd experience a love like that. After I fell from the Light, I figured goodness and love weren't in the cards for me. I mean I'm the freakin' Devil! I thought she'd bolt the second I told her." He chuckled quietly and shook his head. "Imagine my surprise when she stayed."

"You *are* actually an angel, Dad. You're not a monster!" Devlin gave him a small smile as she fought the tears that pricked at her eyes.

"Debatable, but sweet of you, pumpkin." He took a deep breath and continued. "When your mother got sick, I *begged* her to make a deal...to sell her soul to me in exchange for her life, but she refused. She said, '*A soul is too precious to be sold. It's meant to be given to the one you love, not to be bartered like currency. It would cheapen our life and our love if you owned my fate.*" A single tear slid down Damien's cheek. "I cried, I screamed, I tried to bargain, but her mind was made up. There have only ever been two things in all the realms that have held any true meaning to me, and I was completely powerless to save one of them."

"Oh, Dad." Devlin stepped forward to hug him tight as her tears spilled over.

"But you see"—his voice was thick with emotion — "people trade away their souls every day, but not everyone can be bought. Not everyone has a price. Maybe Daniel is one of the special ones. I want you to experience a love like I had. Don't you think it's worth it to find out?"

Devlin's heart warred with her head. She'd never felt this conflicted in her life, but in the end, she couldn't bear feeling that crushing weight of hurt and disappointment if things went sideways again.

"I'm sorry, Dad. I just can't."

CHAPTER TWENTY-EIGHT

This is so weird. Devlin looked at all the empty shelves around her office. Her degrees no longer hung on the wall, and her nameplate had been peeled off the door. The banker box full of crap from her desk was all that had been left for her to pick up. It was an ending and a beginning all wrapped into one neat little package. Devlin had spent the last week tying up the loose ends of her life before her permanent relocation to the Underworld. There had been tears—Kitty's and hers—hugs, and well-wishes from her colleagues. They had naturally assumed that she had either been headhunted to another company or had finally decided to live off daddy's money. Quite frankly, Devlin didn't care what they believed. Effective immediately, she was living by the philosophy that what other people thought of her was none of her damned business. They could have at it!

One last look at the CN Tower then she would jet. Devlin stood at the window and admired the view. There was a light dusting of snow on the ground that sparkled in the bright late-winter sunshine. The Tower rose up majestically between high-rises and office buildings. She would definitely miss this view.

Devlin's peaceful moment was shattered as her office door burst open. With a sigh of annoyance, she turned to greet the intruder, only to be even more irked by what she saw. *What the actual fuck?* Daniel Webster stood in front of her desk, staring at her with wide eyes.

Devlin's heart jumped, but she managed to stuff her feelings back down like a champ. "May I help you?" She patted herself on the back for managing to sound so detached.

Daniel's surprised look made her cold response worth it. "Um, I, ah… I heard through the grapevine that you're moving." He stumbled over his words as his eyes darted around the cleared-out room.

She laid her most unimpressed look on him, despite her breaking heart. "I see that your sense of propriety hasn't changed. Do you harass people without an appointment as a general rule, or am I just lucky?"

"Ah, shit. I'm sorry." Daniel shuffled uncomfortably. "I had to catch you before you left."

"Why is that?" Devlin raised an eyebrow.

"I had to see you. I had to apologize for the things I said to you." He looked desperate.

"That's a shame." Devlin steeled herself, keeping her feet rooted to the floor. "It's just too late."

"It can't be." Daniel stepped toward her and

clasped one of her hands in his. "I've never felt this way with anyone. I can't lose you."

How dare he. Devlin took a steadying breath as she noticed the lights flickering a tad. Where had her magic been when she needed it during training! It figured Daniel would set her off, but it wouldn't do to shatter the light bulbs on her last day. *Time to choose peace, not psychic violence.* She managed to keep her face a mask of calm.

"Go ahead and move. I'll find you. I'll follow you anywhere," Daniel pleaded as he squeezed her hand. "Trust me, I know exactly how creepy and stalkerish that sounded, but I don't care."

Devlin yanked her hand away. "That'll be a bit difficult," she muttered as she dealt with the last couple of items left on her desk. A stress ball. *Figures.* She tossed it into the box. The very last thing was a bound sheaf of paper. She shoved the lid on the box, dropped the paper on top, and picked it up by the handles. Devlin steeled herself and shut off her emotions as she brushed past Daniel. Time seemed to slow, and a shiver ran through her at the fleeting contact. Devlin forced herself to replay the confrontation at Diane's café in her head to stay strong.

As she reached the doorway, she stopped and turned back to face him. "Good luck with the business. I'm sure you'll do great."

Daniel's brow furrowed in confusion. She freed

one hand to slide the paperwork off the box lid. He reached out to take it instinctively, and looked down to see what he'd been handed. Daniel held the ownership paperwork for Harvest Time Garden Market. He stood there opening and closing his mouth in shock, unable to formulate the words he was searching for.

"Goodbye, Daniel." Devlin turned and walked down the hall to the elevators. The heels of her Louboutins clicked on the floor as silent tears slid down her face.

CHAPTER TWENTY-NINE

"Okay, now focus all of your energy on the chair," Craig instructed Devlin as she tried to levitate the damned chair for the thousandth time that day!

Focusing, focusing... The chair is...not moving.

"Damn it!" Devlin growled in frustration as she put her hands on her hips and dropped her head back to stare at the ceiling. "I don't get it! I was a walking magical land mine. Now I can't even make something jiggle!"

Craig started doing a little dance. "Bada bada jiggle, jiggle, it folds..." Craig froze as he caught Devlin's horrified expression. "Stop looking at me like I just farted in church!"

"I'm afraid to ask."

"I guess you don't spend much time on TikTok."

Devlin shook her head no.

Craig chuckled. "Okay, well, we'll just pretend *that* didn't happen! Now, about your magic. Try not to stress about it. It's usually pretty erratic at the beginning. That's totally normal."

"Maybe so, but most people don't go through this in their thirties! It's like magical puberty!" She knew she was being a baby, but she was just too damned frustrated to care.

"Why don't you take a few minutes to re-set and we can give it another go?" He gave her a sympathetic smile and a pat on the back.

Good thinking, Batman. She tried to clear her mind with limited success. She shook her head and started a slow walk around the ballroom that had become her training ground. Devlin's mind wandered as she walked. Things really hadn't worked out too badly for her. She had a gig as an arbitrator, and she was batting one hundred percent on complaint closures. The leaders of the legions were loath to disagree with their boss's daughter. Basically, she had daddy issues, but the good kind!

Devlin shot a sneaky peek at Craig. He had been training her daily, so she'd gotten accustomed to spending time with him, but objectively, Devlin saw how he could weave a web around his prey. The man was sex incarnate. He had romance novel cover-model looks and smelled like he'd jumped out of a Dior cologne ad. There was this alluring, almost shimmery quality to his skin, which just begged to be touched. That was all without using *any* of his incubus mojo. *Leapin' lizards!* How many male movie stars and models were actually incubi living in the human world? Devlin had seriously started trying to figure it out. There had to be a fair few!

"Ready?" Craig shouted from across the room.

Devlin shrugged. "Sure, why not?"

"Why don't we try an exercise to help you focus." Craig dragged another chair over and set both chairs facing each other.

He sat and motioned for Devlin to take the other seat. "It can be hard to connect with our magic if our minds are scattered."

"That hasn't been a problem until recently. My powers used to spew out all over the place. I have no idea why this is happening..." Devlin trailed off as Craig's legs brushed against hers as he man-spread, getting as close to her as he could. Devlin looked into Craig's eyes...big mistake! His irises were a swirling kaleidoscope of color that twisted and morphed faster and faster, snaring her in a semi-hypnotic state. He slid his hands up, letting them come to rest on her shoulders. His scent wrapped around her like a blanket. Devlin started to feel sleepy, or drunk, or maybe both.

"Devlin..." He breathed her name in a deep, raspy voice, full of desire. "I know I shouldn't speak. For all I know, your father will flay me alive in the town square for this, but I had to say something. You're the most alluring creature I've ever met."

While Devlin had seen a hint of Craig's more-than-friendly desires during training, the sudden admission came out of left field. Whatever super-charged lust-inducing magic he was brewing took the edge off her surprise.

"Wow," Devlin mumbled. "That's sweet. You're really hot, and your personality doesn't suck either." She realized she was thinking out loud. "I guess you're after a friends-with-benefits sitch. I mean you're an incubus." She chuckled drunkenly. "You know what though?" She poked him in the chest. "I'm pretty sure you're hitting me with your sextastic pheromones, which is dirty pool, by the way, so I'll hold off answering for a hot minute, if you don't mind."

"Oh shit! I didn't realize..." Craig winced in embarrassment. "It's a bit like a magic boner. If I'm into someone, it can be hard to keep it down. It doesn't happen often, but..." He shrugged.

Devlin gave him a thumbs-up and hoisted her butt off the chair. She was a bit wobbly on her feet, and Craig jumped up just in time to catch her as she swayed forward. The ballroom door opened while he was still holding her upright.

"What the..."

Devlin turned her head toward the sound of the familiar voice, and there he was. Daniel Webster.

She threw off the effect of Craig's sexy whammy in a nanosecond, and her attention was wholly fixed on

Daniel. He was staring at her with longing. His clothes were singed, his hair was smoking just a bit, and a strong smell of sulfur wafted off him.

"Daniel? What are you doing here?" Devlin was in a state of complete shock.

"I told you I'd follow you anywhere," Daniel said as his eyes moved between Devlin and Craig. He nodded slowly. "I'm so stupid. You told me you were done with me. I should have listened."

Devlin squirmed out of Craig's arms and squeezed out from between the chairs as Daniel started mumbling.

"I hope, at the very least, the fact that I came here only to make an ass of myself helps make up for a tiny bit of the hurt I caused you." He started backing toward the door but pointed a finger at Craig. "You treat her right. Don't fuck up like I did. She's special, and she deserves...*everything*." He choked out the last word and turned swiftly, striding out of the room.

CHAPTER THIRTY

Devlin turned to Craig apologetically. "Sorry!" She shrugged and ran out of the ballroom after Daniel. Her brain was firing at a million miles per minute as she caught up with him. *How did he find out about this place? How did he wrap his head around it? Forget all that! How the fuck did he get here?* Her train of thought screeched to a halt the second she flew through the door into the foyer and saw her dad leaning against the banister of the ornate staircase landing. Daniel stood a few feet away looking shell shocked.

Damien wasn't hiding now that he was home. His horns and wings were on full display, and he fixed his darling daughter with a loving gaze from his blood-red eyes. Devlin had to admit no matter what face he was showing, her dad was always a snappy dresser. Getting suits tailored to fit around his majestic, midnight wings was no easy feat, but he made it happen.

Damien smiled. "The young man wanted to have a chat with you and wouldn't take no for an answer." He shrugged. "I even did the *Baphomet head* thing. I figured it would work. Humans don't see a lot of sharp-dressed goats." He gave his daughter a faux innocent smile.

"Dad…" She was *not* playing. "What have you done? How can he be here?"

Damien was suddenly intensely focused on examining his cufflinks. "It was no big deal. I just kldhmaltl…" he mumbled, shifting his eyes to the ceiling.

Her pulse sped up. Something hinky was going on, and nothing good ever came from Damien Laflamme going off-script. Devlin usually found it endearing, but *not* today.

"You did what?"

With an exaggerated sigh, Damien looked his daughter in the eye and enunciated clearly. "I just killed him a little."

"WHAT????"

Daniel had found his voice again, shrieking in unison with Devlin.

"Don't be so dramatic!" Damien rolled his eyes. "He was only dead for a few seconds, and I brought him back…*obviously*." He motioned toward Daniel with a shrug. "He insisted on seeing you, and that was the only way to make him viable for entry. Shuffle off the mortal coil. Side bonus, now that he has technically died, he can visit whenever he wants…being a revenant has its perks!"

"You said I passed out!" Daniel was white as a ghost under the soot.

Damien stepped forward and rested his hands on Daniel's shoulders as he looked him squarely in the eyes. "Son, I'm the Devil. *I lied.*"

"Of course!" Devlin slapped her hand to her forehead. "Revenants can travel above *and* below…the exception to the rule since they've straddled life and death."

"His soul was far to bright and shiny to travel here any other way." Damien walked over and dropped a kiss on her forehead. "Anyhoo, I'll leave you kids to catch up."

Devlin gave her dad a *very* pointed look. "We're going to discuss this later."

"I'm sure we will." Damien gave her a wink and a smile then snapped his fingers and disappeared in an implosion of black smoke. The only sign he'd ever been there was a single black feather that floated down to rest gently on the marble floor. Daniel blinked hard and rubbed his eyes. He noticed the feather and bent down to pick it up, staring at it as though it could give him answers.

"Are you okay?" Devlin asked as she stepped closer to inspect him.

Daniel slid the feather into his pocket and focused on Devlin. He eyed her up and down. "Do you have a tail or horns or something that *you're* hiding?"

The moment was so weird all she could do was

choke on a laugh. "No, I'm half-human, so I guess that canceled out the added bonuses."

"That's something, I guess," Daniel muttered.

"You seem really calm about all of this," Devlin said dubiously.

"Honestly, I think I'm still in shock." He ran a hand through his scorched hair and shuffled nervously. "You're going to have to explain all of this to me. Your father...the freakin' *Devil*—just gave me the CliffsNotes version before he...*killed* me. He didn't even ask first! I find myself really pissed off! He should get a person's sign-off first before just going around killing folks."

The shock was clearly wearing off. "What are you doing here, Daniel? Traveling all the way to Hell for a chat seems a bit extreme."

"Well, like I said before, I'd follow you anywhere, though I didn't realize *this* was a possibility." He sighed. "I know you don't want anything to do with me romantically, and I get that, but there are things I need to tell you," he said as he walked toward her. He reached out for her instinctively then caught himself, dropping his hand back down to his side. "You deserve the whole story."

"There are things I need to tell you too. Clearly..." Devlin looked into Daniel's eyes and saw resignation. "Let me get the staff to show you to a shower and get you a change of clothes first. You look a little crispy around the edges."

Daniel nodded gratefully. "A shower would be amazing. I feel like I've been dragged through a volcano, torn apart at the molecular level, and pummeled by a Golden Gloves boxer."

"You're not far off," Devlin muttered.

He held up his hands and shook his head. "I don't want to know."

Devlin walked over to the wall and tugged on a bell-pull to summon the butler. "Let's get you sorted out. Then we can meet up in the drawing room in an hour or so."

Whatever he had to tell her *had* to be important. Maybe not important enough to die for—since her dad hadn't exactly been transparent with that little detail—but important enough to go to Hell and back.

CHAPTER THIRTY-ONE

The drawing room was Devlin's favorite place in the palace. There were a pair of stuffed velvet chairs by a large window that had the best view of Limbo she'd seen yet. She couldn't quite believe that Daniel was here, in the Underworld, that he was in her home. If she was honest with herself, her hurt had never really stopped her from wanting him. Now, here he was, showing up looking like a piece of crispy bacon. She was as nervous as...well...her dad in church. Her heart was racing, and her fickle thoughts kept turning to Daniel's lips dancing with hers and their hands exploring each other's bodies. Her temperature was rising like she'd spent an hour in a Hellfire sauna.

The sound of hooves clicking on the hard flooring in the hallway drew her attention away from her increasingly naughty thoughts.

A knock sounded on the door. "Come in," Devlin called out.

The door swung open to reveal a tuxedoed Satyr. "Master Daniel, madam." He stepped aside and motioned for Daniel to enter.

Devlin smiled graciously. "Thank you, Lycus."

Daniel stepped past Lycus; his eyes were wide in disbelief. "Thanks for showing me the way...sir?" He gave the Satyr a nervous smile.

Lycus just stared up at him, supremely unimpressed, and bleated. Devlin burst out laughing as Daniel jumped and hurried into the room. Lycus smiled at Devlin and gave her a wink before he bowed formally and stepped back into the hallway.

"So, what other mythological creatures are real?" Daniel asked as he sat down across from Devlin.

"If you've heard a story about them, they probably exist." Devlin leaned in and stage whispered, "You've probably run into demons before too. Lots of them live among mortals, working day jobs and paying taxes."

Daniel's eyebrows shot up. "Really?"

"Oh yeah! I mean, *politicians*..." She burst out laughing as Daniel nodded, seemingly unsurprised. "But seriously, Craig has been my dad's assistant for years, and I had no idea he was an incubus! It's not easy to tell. Well, it wasn't easy to tell before. Lately I've been able to sense them."

Daniel shifted uncomfortably at the mention of Craig. "I knew this was a long shot, and I was clearly right. You and *Craig* seemed pretty close earlier."

Devlin shook her head. "Craig is my trainer, so there's no need to get spicy about him."

Daniel looked relieved. "So, he's a trainer like... for the gym?"

"Not quite. He's helping me learn how to use and control my magic, which has gone completely AWOL for some unknown reason." Devlin sighed with renewed frustration.

"Right, demons...magic...Before your father decided to scare the living shit out of me, I thought he was joking. I mean, the *Devil*?" Daniel started to babble. "I figured he was cosplaying or something, but method-acting cosplay, cosplay two-point-oh. Not that he seems like the role-playing type."

"He always had the best costume out of all the dads at Halloween." Devlin shrugged, hoping Daniel's rambling didn't mean his brain was starting to cave in.

Daniel nodded. "I bet." He tilted his chin toward the window. "That sure wasn't what I had imagined Hell would be look like, ...not that I spent a lot of time imagining Hell. I certainly never imagined I'd be here."

"Me neither."

Daniel gave her a questioning look. "What do you mean?"

"I came here for the first time a few weeks ago. Dad told me stories, but nothing compares to seeing the place in person. It's actually quite beautiful in its own way."

"You're right, it is." Daniel looked a bit stunned at his admission. "Wait, how can you be the daughter of the Devil but not have visited his…kingdom?" he asked.

"That's the stuff that I need to explain. To be clear, when we met, I didn't quite realize what was happening, but I had just started tapping into my magic for the first time." She fiddled with her watch nervously. "To enter the Underworld, you have to be *of* the Underworld. I appeared to be mortal, so no entry."

Damien looked like he was trying to solve the Goldbach Conjecture. "The radio…the exploding lights…the fire?"

Devlin nodded solemnly.

"So, you're actually magic!" Daniel's face lit up. "Maybe I'm losing it, but that's actually pretty fucking cool."

She smiled nervously as her heart fluttered. She couldn't let herself go back down this road. "You said you had things to tell me?" she asked him.

"Yes. Let me try to explain why I acted like such an epic asshole." He reached out and took her hands, squeezing them gently.

It won't change anything. Devlin sighed, but at the same time, it wouldn't kill her to hear him out.

"Go ahead."

Daniel took a deep breath and began. "I was with

someone for a few years, Amy. Actually, we were engaged. I thought everything was good, but she was hooking up with one of my brothers, Chad, behind my back." Daniel shifted uncomfortably in his seat. "Amy wanted to go on fancy trips and be seen at the right restaurants. I must have really disappointed her when I became a family law attorney and did a lot of pro-bono work. She probably assumed I would become a corporate attorney for a Fortune Five Hundred company and be making it rain."

Ding, ding, ding. There's the reason he hates corporate attorneys.

Daniel stood and started pacing as he continued. "Chad was more aligned with her lifestyle choices. He liked clothes, cars, and having his photo in society magazines. The two of them together were a menace. They concocted a plan to get me disinherited. With so many siblings, I guess Chad figured one less heir would increase his share a bit. Who knew if he was planning on working cons to screw our other siblings too. Maybe he wasn't the mastermind, maybe it was Amy, but either way, they destroyed my life." Daniel walked to the window and stared out over the city. "They made it look like I had defrauded the family trust. Amy made up outlandish stories about how horrible I was to her. My father started to question everything I did, everything I said. I couldn't believe he would swallow all those lies. I left the country to clear my head and kept extending my trip. I guess part of me didn't want to come back and see that look of disappointment on his face again."

Devlin listened in shock. No wonder Diane had warned her not to hurt him. He'd been through a meat grinder!

"I was out of touch with the whole family… everyone I knew at home, actually. When I finally decided to come back, I found out my father had passed away." Daniel hung his head in shame. "He died disappointed in me, believing the worst of me."

Devlin could almost feel Daniel's heart breaking again as he relived his story. Her body seemed to move of its own volition. She felt that familiar sense of being drawn to him, and she was at his side in the space between seconds.

Daniel started as she appeared beside him. "What the fuck!"

"Did I just…" Devlin stood rooted to the spot with wide eyes.

"Do the *poof* thing your father does? Yeah! That was actually pretty cool." Daniel gave her a look of admiration. "You're kinda like a superhero, aren't you?"

"Okay, I'm more freaked out than you are! You're an odd bird, Daniel Webster!"

He looked excited suddenly. "Your superhero name needs to be…The Litigator…no, Super Counsel…

Oh wait! I've got it! Legal Eagle!" They both groaned at that one.

"Ha!" Devlin laughed. "Well, sorry for interrupting you with my unplanned magic show. Please tell me the rest." She reached out and touched his arm gently.

Devlin could tell the exact moment Daniel's thoughts reconnected to his family drama. A cloud drifted over his face, and the tiny sparkle that had lit his eye vanished.

"I came back to fix things with my father, but all that was left was saving his legacy. When Chad told me the sale had gone through and that you were named as the purchaser, my head went straight back to what he and Amy had done. I just assumed you'd been out to screw me…in more ways than one. I shouldn't have let my past get in the way, but by the time I cooled down and sorted my shit out, it was too late."

"Oh, Daniel, I wish I had known…" Devlin looked up at him as they stood side-by-side with the twilight of Limbo as a backdrop.

He shrugged and looked into her eyes. "If you had known, it still wouldn't have excused the way I treated you. I know I've probably irreparably blown it, but you're it for me, Devlin. I'll follow you anywhere, for all of time, if you'll let me."

The sincerity and longing radiated off of him, but

there was still something bugging her. Why *had* he taken an interview with Obsidian's biggest competitor?

"What was the deal with you interviewing at Voyager Industries then?"

Daniel suddenly looked guilty as sin. "I was too wrapped up in my own bullshit to talk to you, but I still had to see you. I figured if I worked at a competitor, we would run into each other at times. I needed you in my life, even if it was just to fight over contracts again."

Devlin's eyebrows shot up in her shock. "I thought you were giving me the professional middle finger, but you're really just a masochist!"

Daniel face-palmed himself. "I've really bolloxed this whole thing up in spectacular fashion, haven't I?"

"Fittingly, it's a Hellish mess," Devlin agreed as they laughed together.

"Please give me another chance." Daniel stood before her, his heart and his hurt laid bare.

Devlin could feel *her* heart pounding out of her chest. "I...I want to, I really do...but there are other issues to think of now. I can't have my heart broken again." She said, as the organ in question cramped at the thought of walking away from Daniel again.

"Other issues? There's *more*?" Daniel joked. "Just kidding. Please tell me."

Devlin let out a sad chuckle. "I'm Nephil, a cross between human and angel. We have no idea what that's going to mean for me…for my future. If I'm mortal or immortal like my dad. There's just so much we don't know. I can't expect a mortal to stick around. At this point, uncertainty just keeps on coming, and what doesn't kill me makes me weirder and harder to relate to."

"So, let me get this straight." Daniel looked at her very seriously. "You're a real-life, honest-to-goodness, magic angel… I could have told you that weeks ago!"

Devlin's heart melted. All the stress she'd been holding on to drained out of her.

Daniel reached out to cup her cheek. "Whatever happens, we can face it together. All I know is that I've never felt this away about anybody. There's a gaping hole in my life when you're gone, so letting you walk away again isn't an option. Whether I get fifty minutes or fifty years, I'll take it. Anything is better than another moment without you."

"Well then…" Devlin stepped into Daniel, close enough that their bodies brushed gently. "I think any man willing to follow me into the Underworld, who can wrap their head around my dad being the Devil, and who thinks my weird abilities are super hero-esque is worth a second chance."

A relieved breath whooshed out of Daniel. "Oh, thank G—" He caught himself in the nick of time and gave Devlin a wry smile.

Devlin raised herself up on her toes and threw her arms around him. Her heart was full to bursting as their lips met in a kiss full of future and promise. The candles in every sconce and candelabra flamed to life. Magic burst from her body like a mini nuclear blast. The shockwave rolled through the palace and out into the streets, their passion igniting Limbo with sparks and light.

CHAPTER THIRTY-TWO

Devlin could certainly get on board with spring in North Bay. It was beautiful, and she could feel her extremities at all times. They had finally come full circle. The relationship started with Harvest Time, and here they were, back again. Her permanent move to the balmy climes of Limbo had been kiboshed in favor of a cabin and Danny Webster. They planned on making regular trips to Limbo, but some intense training with Craig before they'd portalled out had definitely helped her get control of her powers. Some couples were bi-coastal; they were bi-dimensional. Daniel was definitely the key to her Nephil magic. He tapped into her emotions like no other. Surprisingly, Daniel and Craig seemed to be living a dream bromance built on a foundation of hockey and beer.

Devlin was just happy to be in a place where she didn't have to be angry or horny to use her magic, and the *vanishing in a puff of smoke* thing really was the cat's ass. She may have used it once or twice to beat Daniel to the bedroom.

Despite the rocky start, Devlin and Daniel were giving coupledom a go. *So far, so good.* Damien had looked far too pleased with himself when he'd heard the news. He gloated like he'd single-handedly brought the whole relationship to pass, which was kind of true, but Devlin would never admit it to her dad. It would make him impossible!

Daniel had done a lot of damage control with the staff at Harvest Time. They were starting to come around now that they were meeting the real Daniel Webster...and rumor at the water cooler was that, as a boss, he was a lot like his father. Today was the day they would finally go through George Webster's office. It had been locked up tight since his passing. Despite all their faults, his siblings hadn't brought themselves to clean it out either. Daniel still wasn't in a forgiving headspace when it came to Chad, but never say never.

Devlin was wrapping up the knickknacks from the top of one of the cabinets, while Daniel went through boxes of files stacked against the wall. She'd found a rhythm with the packing. Pick up an item, roll it in the bubble wrap, tape, then box, item, bubble wrap, tape, box, item, bubble... *Wait, what's that?* Devlin heard a clinking noise from inside the little ceramic jar in her hand. Curious, she tipped it over, and out slid a key.

"Daniel!" She rushed over to him, her eyes wide with excitement as she held it up.

He dropped the file folder he was holding and grabbed it. "Oh wow! Do you think that's the key for the locked drawer?"

"Wanna give it a go?" Devlin's inner Nancy Drew was clamoring to solve the mystery.

Daniel was already at the desk. "Twist my rubber arm!"

"Ready?" He nodded and slid the key home.

Daniel turned the key, and they heard the lock snick open. He grabbed the handle of the drawer and pulled. The only thing inside was a white envelope addressed to Daniel.

"That's my father's handwriting." He stared at it like it was a grenade with the pin pulled.

"I can't." He turned to Devlin with a desperate look. "Can you read it first, just…let me know how bad it is."

"Are you sure?" she asked as she reached into the drawer and picked up the envelope.

Daniel nodded and started fidgeting with his glasses. Devlin slid her finger under the lip of the envelope and tore it open. There was a single page of spidery writing folded inside. She took a breath and began to read to herself. She stopped a few lines in.

"Daniel, you really need to read this yourself." She held the letter out to him.

He shook his head. "Just tell me what it says."

Devlin re-opened the letter and read it aloud. "'My dearest son Daniel. I don't have the words to express how deeply sorry I am for having doubted your integrity. I know now that Chad and Amy abused my trust and impugned your character horribly in an effort to acquire a larger share of the family trust. Please know that I have not made any amendments to exclude you, or anyone, from any inheritance. Despite his abominable behavior, Chad is still my son, and I cannot leave him wanting. I know you will understand. It saddens me that I will not be able to say these things to you in person. You deserve far more than a letter after our last conversation, but unfortunately, time is not on my side. You will make a success of whatever you set your mind to, my son. You have always had a clear vision of who you are, what you want, and what you stand for. Be happy. Life is short, but beautiful. My one regret is not being able to say goodbye. I love you, son.'"

Devlin could hardly believe the change in Daniel as she finished the letter and folded it back into its envelope. He looked like the weight of the world had been lifted off his shoulders. Daniel took the envelope and placed it on the desk. A tear rolled down his cheek and past his maddening crooked smile as he grabbed her into his arms and kissed her deeply.

"Everything is just right," he said as he pulled back to look Devlin in the eye. "This is the first day of the rest of my life, and there is nobody I want with me on this journey more than you, Devlin Laflamme. I'm Hell bent on loving you!"

"Sounds like a good plan to me." Devlin reached up to trace a finger along his jawline, then let her hand drop down to rest over his heart.

Daniel's eyes darkened with passion, and she felt her body respond immediately. This man was absolutely made for her. With a wicked smile, Devlin reached out with her magic. The office door swung closed with a thud.

"Handy." Daniel winked.

"Wanna break a few company policies?" she asked.

"Hell yes! Rules *were* made to be broken after all!" Daniel pulled her body flush against his, letting her feel just how badly he wanted to throw out the rule book.

Devlin slid a hand around his neck, spearing her fingers into his hair. "So, who's in charge this time, Mister Webster?"

"Flip a coin?" he suggested as he dipped his head down to press his lips against hers.

With a snap of her fingers, the overhead lights turned off. *Game on!*